The Buccaneer
AND THE BLUESTOCKING

The Culpepper Misses, Book Four

COLLETTE CAMERON

Blue Rose Romance®

Sweet-to-Spicy Timeless Romance®

THE BUCCANEER AND THE BLUESTOCKING
Copyright © 2018 Collette Cameron
All Rights Reserved

Cover Design by: Angela Archer, Long Valley Designs LLC

Attn: Permissions Coordinator
Blue Rose Romance®
P.O. Box 167, Scappoose, OR 97056

ISBN Paperback: 9781954307339
ISBN eBook: 9781954307322
collettecameron.com

He opened those incredibly dark eyes,
and for an instant, she was lost in their depths—
a connection she couldn't put words to
holding her fast and quickening her pulse.

"Entertaining Regency romance full of humor,
forbidden attraction, & intrigue."
~Anna Campbell, author of the bestselling
Dashing Widows series

Other Collette Cameron Books

The Culpepper Misses
The Earl and the Spinster
The Marquis and the Vixen
The Lord and the Wallflower
The Buccaneer and the Bluestocking
The Lieutenant and the Lady

Check out Collette's Other Series
Castle Brides
Highland Heather Romancing a Scot
Daughters of Desire (Scandalous Ladies)
The Honorable Rogues®
Seductive Scoundrels
Heart of a Scot

Dedication

For MKS
Miss you.

Acknowledgements

So many people were involved in the writing of *The Buccaneer and the Bluestocking*, and they all must be acknowledged.

Thank you, Maxine Wilson for suggesting M'Lady Lottie's name, and to Nicole Laverdure for your expertise in translating the French in Blaike and Oliver's story. Sharon Fornier and Courtney Chase, your contributions to M'Lady Lottie's colorful vocabulary were priceless.

Star Montgomery, a special thanks to you for answering all of my cockatoo questions and even sharing a recording of Koo Koo, your cockatoo. Thanks too, to Linda Martin for sending along the adorable talking parrot video which gave me the idea to teach M'Lady Lottie animal sounds.

Of course, I must give a shout out to Kathryn Lynn Davis for her fabulous edits. Oh, and to Anna Campbell for *The Buccaneer and the Bluestocking's* cover quote too. Lastly, I'd be remiss if I didn't acknowledge my assistants DF and CJ for the myriad of things they do to help me and keep me sane!

xoxo

A lady of refinement takes utmost
care to consider that every word whispered in
confidence 'tis oft' heard repeated many miles away.
~*Scruples and Scandals*
The Genteel Lady's Guide to Practical Living

Port de Lyon, Lyon, France
Early Evening 17 March, 1823

A stuffed-to-its-capacity portmanteau in one hand, and a small sack of food in the other, Blaike inhaled a fortifying breath as she stepped from the rickety coach. A brow raised, half in relief and half in wariness, she surveyed *Port de Lyon's* bustling wharf.

Situated at the intersections of the *Saône* and *Rhône* rivers, the busy harbor hummed with activity. All sorts of vehicles rumbled to and fro, while merchants huffed past, their covered carts containing coveted silks and other treasures.

Vendors enthusiastically hawked their wares alongside street urchins and beggars haranguing passersby for a coin or two. Stevedores and gruff seamen of every nationality called to each other above the din as they loaded and unloaded cargo. Others drunkenly staggered along, leering at or propositioning the few women braving the docks at this hour.

Except for the Culpeppers, a male or a stern-faced chaperone accompanied any other ladies of gentle breeding, distinguishing the respectable females on the wharf from the doxies beginning their work as twilight's mantle descended.

Despite the impropriety and the thorough scolding they'd receive when they reached home, Blaike and Blaire had journeyed to Lyon and would sail to England unchaperoned. They had much explaining to do to their family upon arriving home.

No, rather Madame Beaulieu, proprietress and head mistress of *Les Dames de l'Académie de Grâce,* had much to account for.

The deceptive, conniving witch.

Institute for higher education, indeed.

What utter poppycock and claptrap.

Les Dames de l'Académie de Grâce was nothing but a glorified finishing school. Which, Blaike strongly suspected, doubled as a brothel. Far too many unexplainable comings and goings by men visiting the other house on the property at all hours.

A shudder rippled down her spine that had nothing to do with the brisk March air.

Several laughing or jabbering French sailors in crisp blue and gold uniforms hurried past as her twin Blaire, came to Blaike's side.

Blaike only understood a smattering of their words, but what she did comprehend heated her cheeks.

One debonair officer with a pencil-thin black mustache, winked, while another tossed a pastry scrap to a pair of hungry-looking mongrels.

Teeth bared, they snarled and snapped, each vying for the largest share.

Poor beasts.

She'd experienced hunger; was experiencing it at this moment, as a matter of fact. To stretch their swiftly dwindling funds, she and Blaire had shared their two meager meals a day, and neither had eaten since breaking their fast with tea and toast at dawn. Scant money remained in the reticule hanging from Blaike's wrist; a worry that cramped her stomach worse than lack of food.

Blaire's purse held little more.

The rolls, cheese, and apples Blaike had purchased from the inn this morning would have to suffice until they boarded the ship home. Pray God they sailed soon. If not . . .

A distinguished looking man—a ship's captain from his attire and confident bearing—descended a gangplank and was met by several other finely dressed gentlemen awaiting him on the waterfront. He slashed a casual glance in Blaike's direction, then brazenly pivoted to more fully observe her. A slow smile curved his mouth, crinkling the scar lancing his left cheek as he stared.

He doffed his brown leather Continental hat and inclined his head.

At once, the others turned to see what had captured his attention.

A rotund fellow wearing a gaudy canary-yellow coat boldly withdrew his quizzing glass and put it to his eye.

Ridiculous. As if he could see them any better through the lens that far away.

When the captain, or whomever he was, continued to regard Blaike and Blaire, his mien almost speculative, she angled her back toward him. In her limited experience, men misinterpreted even the most casual of glances as an invitation.

Besides, the last time her nape hair had stood at attention in this manner, she'd been brutally accosted. After tucking the food beneath her arm, she switched her heavy valise to her other hand and pressed her palm to her hollow midriff.

An assortment of noxious smells hung heavily in the air, and Blaike wrinkled her nose before releasing a slow, gusty sigh.

"Lord, it reeks most awfully." Blaire raised a slightly soiled gloved hand to her nose. "What is that stench? Rotting fish and—?"

"I'm not sure, but I agree. It's most disgusting. But at least with the breeze the air is slightly fresher than the fusty interior of the coach." Barely. Blaike arched her spine, stretching the stiff muscles from bum to neck. "I swear, someone let a billy goat live in that conveyance."

"Maybe Brette's grandfather, old Fusty Boots, used it a decade or so ago." Blaire chuckled as she, too, examined the pier. Their cousin's grandsire, the Duke of Bellinghamshire's malodorous feet had been legendary.

Three and a half days they'd rattled about in the stinking, poorly sprung equipage. Why, even now whilst standing, Blaike could yet feel the rhythmic jostling. Flattened from constant wear, the seat provided minimal padding against the jolts and bumps. She'd be surprised if a spot remained on her or Blaire's bodies that didn't sport bruises.

Although . . .

Not all of her welts could be blamed upon the

poorly sprung, well-used coach.

She closed her eyes for an agonizing instant, remembering—

"*Zut.*"

The sour-tempered driver swore beneath his breath, and she glanced over her shoulder, wincing when he hauled their small trunk from the boot and dropped it on the ground with the same distaste as a sack of weevil-infested grain.

He'd been miffed since the first day and the vails he'd expected hadn't been forthcoming. As much as Blaike would've liked to have passed him a coin or two, their dire circumstances required her to economize at every opportunity.

"*Odeur putride,*" he grumbled.

Indeed. Most putrid.

Wrinkling his nose, he swore again. "*Merde. Le navire esclave est au port.*"

"Did he say a slave ship is in port?" Blaire's gaze flew to the rows of towering masts lining the gloaming sky.

"I shudder to think so." Blaike opened her eyes. Queasiness tensed her stomach even as the vile odor clogged her throat. "God help them."

"But I thought slavery had been abolished in France." After tossing Blaike a distressed look, Blaire scrutinized the ships nearest them as if she sought to see the pathetic wretches confined inside the stout hulls.

"It was, but I remember reading somewhere the ban hasn't fully taken effect yet."

The twins situation paled compared to those desperate souls so brutally torn from their home and everything familiar.

At least she and Blaire more or less knew what their futures held.

Just over a month ago, when the situation at the academy had deteriorated to intolerable, Blaike had secretly written and posted a letter to her sister, Blythe, Marchioness of Leventhorpe. She'd asked her to arrange passage home as hastily as possible and said she would explain the reasons later. Suspecting Madame Beaulieu steamed the wax seals loose and read their correspondences, Blaike had asked Blythe to respond in code.

In her reply, Blythe was to mention a date for a house party and that would be the day they were to sail. Too dangerous to name the ship, but she'd say the arrangements had all been made, or something of that nature.

Though Blaike and Blaire had already planned on leaving later in the spring when the weather improved, a recent incident had compelled their immediate departure.

'Flight' more aptly described their leave-taking.

Blaike didn't know how they'd have managed if it weren't for Blythe's generosity—or rather her husband's—and her assurance their passage had been arranged. She and Blaire were to inquire at *Port de Lyon's* Harbor Master's Office regarding the matter.

"Blaike?" Worry roughened Blaire's soft voice around the edges.

"Yes, dearest?"

"What if the ship we're to sail upon isn't in port yet? We are nearly a fortnight earlier than the date Blythe gave us."

It didn't bear contemplating, for the coach and lodging from Geneva had exhausted the monies they'd managed to secret away at the academy these past wretched months.

She could always try to sell their clothing and few pieces of jewelry, though the gems had been gifts from their guardian, the Earl of Ravensdale. True, their garments were of the finest quality and the latest fashion, but they hadn't many with them. They'd escaped the school in such a rush, that the bulk of their possessions were left behind along with instructions where to ship them.

Honestly, cows were more likely to crow than

either she or Blaire were ever to see their belongings again. Madame Beaulieu would claim the lot as her due for some fabricated reason or other. The woman hadn't a virtuous or honest bone in her skeletally thin body.

Offering Blaire a reassuring smile, more forced confidence than actual bravado, Blaike searched for the Port Captain's Office. "All will be well, I'm sure of it. I feel it in my bones. We've come this far, and surely we deserve a little grace after enduring more mishaps than a Greek tragedy—"

"A broken wheel, a fallen tree, a lame horse, and a flooded creek." Blaire held up three fingers, then a fourth, followed shortly by a fifth. "Required to sleep leaning against one another in a common room that second night. Not to mention I'm hungry enough to lick crumbs from a biscuit tin, and our driver has the temperament of a wounded—"

"Bear." They were forever finishing one another's sentences.

"He is most surly, even though we've done our utmost not to inconvenience him." To ease the pinching between her shoulder blades, Blaike rolled her shoulders.

"True." Blaire shook her blond head, the once crisp silk flowers adorning her hat flopping with the motion. She slipped her hand into the crook of Blaike's elbow.

"We have each other though," she said, giving her twin a little hug. "I know we'll manage somehow."

"This is all my fault." Blaike pressed her lips together and dragged in another deep breath. "I'm truly sorry, Blaire."

Tears tingled, but she blinked them away. The time for remorse had passed. Wallowing in regret and self-pity wouldn't help now.

Balancing her hat boxes while making a comforting noise in her throat, Blaire slipped her arm around Blaike's waist. "Stuff and nonsense, dear one." She leaned into her sister's side. "And know this, Blaike. Your secret will always be safe with me. I shall never, *ever* breathe a word. If anyone is to know the whole of it, you will do the telling, not I."

Those dratted, stubborn tears welled again, and Blaike swallowed. Mortification burned to her marrow. "I know. And I trust you. But we aren't the only ones who know what transpired. Should it become public knowledge, our entire family will be—."

"Shamed." Sternness tightened Blaire's pretty features briefly. "Perhaps, but it was not of your doing," she insisted. "I believe, even when dark secrets are exposed, honorable and decent people can rise above the gossip and stigma."

Easier said when you weren't the one nearly

despoiled and caught dishabille by Madame Beaulieu. Never mind that Blaike had been the victim of a calculated scheme, and that was why she'd determined never to be manipulated into doing anything against her will again.

Despite her protests of innocence, she'd been judged, tried, and found guilty by the headmistress in mere moments. Compromised beyond redemption, her reputation and good standing utterly tattered, remaining at *Les Dames de l'Académie de Grâce* had been inconceivable.

Much too convenient the headmistress happening upon Blaike in the gardens just then.

Why, the despicable woman had implied Blaike had no recourse other than to become a courtesan. Another reason why Blaike suspected Madame Beaulieu was an entirely other kind of *madam*.

"God forgive me, but I truly loathe Jonathon and Jacqueline Severs," Blaike whispered. "And Madame Beaulieu isn't far behind. They should all face imprisonment."

"Vile, all three to their foul cores." Blaire tapped Blaike's forearm.

"But, think on it. We aren't likely to ever lay eyes on the Severs again. They're American, from a banking family, I believe Jacqueline said. And if we do, I'll be the first to cork Jonathon Severs for you. In fact, I think I'll take pugilist lessons. Fencing too." She skewed her mouth sideways. "I suppose I'll have to get Heath's permission, since he's our guardian. That's a bit of a bother."

She struck a pose, her fist poised before her face, and giggled. "Do you think he'll—?"

"Agree? Not likely."

"*Mademoiselles.*" Again, the contentious driver harrumphed behind them.

Blaike and Blaire swung to face the peevish man.

"*Capitaine de Port de Sa Majesté.*" He pointed to an official looking building a block down and across the way before towing their trunk to plop it beside them.

He couldn't have stopped the conveyance in front of the building?

Plain spiteful, that.

Surely he didn't expect them to haul the chest themselves? The trunk was far too heavy and cumbersome. Besides, they each already held a portmanteau, and Blaire also carried two hat boxes. Furthermore, with the riff raff scuttling about the docks, they daren't leave the trunk unattended.

"Port Captain? Har-bor Mas-ter?"

Blaike pointed at the building, and Blaire frowned at the trunk. Neither had learned enough French to communicate well during their ill-fated venture.

"*Oui*." Mouth turned down, their driver summoned a sullen nod.

Blaike mentally calculated her funds again.

Could she spare a coin or two?

Her tense stomach cinched further. She had no choice.

After drawing her reticule off her wrist, and setting their meager food supply upon the chest, she loosened the strap.

"*Pardonnez-moi, mais puis-je vous offrir mon aide?*"

Use caution in befriending those who whisper
secrets to each other in your presence. You can bet
they'll not hesitate to titter about you as well.
~*Scruples and Scandals*
The Genteel Lady's Guide to Practical Living

2

Blaike started and glanced up to see the man approaching who'd been watching her and Blaire earlier. Perhaps late in his fourth decade or early in his fifth, he bestowed a cavalier's smile upon them as he sketched a bow.

Three burly sailors accompanied him, each more coarse and intimidating in appearance than the former.

Making a pretense of returning her reticule to her wrist, she eyed the trio from beneath her lashes. What she observed didn't reassure her.

The first, an enormous African his bulging muscles straining against the fabric of his partially unbuttoned shirt, grinned widely, revealing missing front teeth. The second, perhaps a Turk or Arab given his soiled cranberry-colored turban, fingered the hilt of a wicked looking saber belted at his waist. And the third seaman sported a long, braided beard and numerous tattoos on every exposed inch of flesh, including his face.

She didn't want to speculate what the rest of the crew was like if these three were the captain's officers. Never having seen pirates before, she couldn't be sure, of course, but these rapscallions fit every depiction she'd ever read.

Right down to the gold hoop in the Turk's ear.

Blaire must have reached the same conclusion, for she edged minutely closer to Blaike.

A prickly shudder skittered across Blaike's shoulders.

A renewed reminder why young women didn't travel unescorted.

Her nostrils quivered.

A most unsavory—*unbathed*—lot.

Except for their leader.

Flawlessly groomed—*togs of the first stare of fashion* as she'd heard dandies described in London— he oozed charm as well as a faint, musky cologne.

Attractive in an experienced, man-of-the-world manner, he wasn't overly tall. In fact, she and Blaire each stood at least an inch taller. Nonetheless, he still exuded power and self-confidence. The scar lashing his face suited him in a bizarre sort of way.

How had he come by it?

He rather looked like a Barbary Pirate or corsair more than a respectable ship's captain.

A similar thought had sprung to mind the first time she'd seen Captain Oliver Whitehouse.

Truth to tell, she'd had many fanciful thoughts about Captain Whitehouse these past months.

The leader spoke again. *"Est-ce que je peux vous aider avec vos bagages?"*

Not exactly certain what he'd asked, Blaike believed he might've offered to assist with their luggage. "Please pardon me, but I do not speak French fluently."

A delighted smile brightened his face, and he clasped one hand across his waist as he bent into an elegant bow.

"Splendid. You're British, as am I. I was but offering my assistance with your baggage." He gestured to the chest. "Please permit my men carry it to wherever you might need." He glanced, almost too casually given his hand resting on the carved handle of a knife tucked into his waistband. "Have you any other luggage? Perhaps a tardy traveling companion's as well?"

Fishing for information, that.

He'd find his probing wouldn't get satisfied.

Blaike wasn't born yesterday. Pure foolishness to

reveal that no fire-breathing dragon such as Mrs. Hobbs, their chaperone on the passage from London, would join them shortly. And the lady's maids who'd accompanied them from London had been sent home within a week of arrival.

Madam Beaulieu didn't condone her pupils being waited upon, most especially when other attendees didn't have abigails.

After withdrawing a few francs from his coat pocket, the captain passed them to the waiting driver.

"*Merci beaucoup.*" The surly bear's demeanor transformed into grateful servitude. He tapped two fingers to his forehead in a smart salute before shutting the coach door and climbing atop the seat. A moment later, the vehicle trundled away.

Exchanging a resigned glance with her twin, Blaike stifled a sigh and forced her lips to bend upward into a grateful smile.

"Thank you for your kindness. We're going just there."

She indicated the Harbor Master's Office.

"Quaco. Demir." The stranger picked up the food sack, then sliced his other hand at two of his gargantuan men, indicating they should lift the trunk.

The African and Easterner did so with pathetic ease.

"Eades, carry the ladies valises."

Definitely a man accustomed to giving orders and having them promptly obeyed.

"Aye, Captain," Eades said in a thick accent Blaike didn't recognize. He extended his dirty, chipped-nail hand for Blaike's portmanteau, his lecherous gaze dropping to her bosoms.

Blaike reluctantly passed him her bag, as did Blaire with even less enthusiasm.

She hugged her hatboxes close to her chest, however. "I'll carry these."

Clutching their food bag in a fist, the stranger extended his elbows. He clearly expected Blaike and Blaire to take either arm.

"Sir, while we do appreciate you and your crew's gallantry, it would, nonetheless, be most unseemly to take your arm when we've not been properly introduced." Blaike slid Blaire a sideways glance.

Something akin to distress flashed in her twin's sapphire eyes.

So, she feels it, too.

Unease flooded Blaike at being obligated to him.

Annoyance cast a fleeting shadow over his face, hardening his craggy features for an instant. Just as swiftly, his peevishness disappeared, and he produced another amiable smile, the warmth not quite reflecting in his glacial pale blue gaze.

Then, at their continued hesitation, he nodded, approval pleating the corners of his eyes. "Most wise to be cautious, especially when you're traveling alone. I am Landon Abraham, captain of the *Black Dove,* and citizen of London when I'm not at sea."

Was it her imagination, or did he have the very slightest of accents? Was he truly British, then?

For certain, Blaike didn't want him to know no chaperone would accompany them, but neither could she lie outright. At the moment, she wasn't sure her inability to tell a taradiddle without giving herself away was a strength or a curse.

What to do?

Perhaps a fellow female passenger—a married woman—might be persuaded to assume the role if promised payment once they reached London. Yes, indeed that might suffice quite well. It wouldn't exactly be a lie to say they'd meet their companion on the ship. Surely others had booked passage as well. If naught else, they'd be traveling companions for the voyage's duration.

"Our companion and her husband are to meet us aboard the vessel." That clever husband bit just popped into her mind.

Blaike slid Blaire a telling look.

Comprehension dawned, and her twin's eyes rounded.

"Indeed, they will. Our guardian always insists on the most respectable of chaperones." She nodded a trifle too enthusiastically while shifting her hatboxes.

An immense emerald-cut ruby ring glinting on his forefinger, Captain Abraham scratched his jaw. "Excellent. All manner of motley scoundrels roam *Port de Lyon's* wharf. You can never be too cautious, Miss . . .?"

Again, a hint as broad as an old dairy cow's behind.

If Blaike refused an introduction, she'd seem surly and ungrateful. Perhaps, however, revealing her peerage connections would detour any unwanted attention or misplaced notions he might have.

"I am Blaike Culpepper, and this is my sister, Blaire. Our cousin, Brooke, is married to Heath, Earl of Ravensdale. He is also our guardian. Our sister Blythe is wed to Tristan, Marquis of Leventhorpe, and we've another cousin, Brette, who is Alexander, Earl of Wycombe's wife."

Dash it all. That sounded more like an uppity boast than a deterrent.

An unabashed grin tipped the captain's lips. "You've quite a number of unusual names, and all beginning with Bs. Does it ever get confusing?"

"Yes. Often." A common occurrence, and something the Culpeppers had to explain time and again. "Unfortunately, our mothers continued a family tradition wherein the female offspring all receive names beginning with Bs."

Blaire piped up. "But Mama and Aunt Bess took it a step further and exercised what little power women of their generation had by selecting gender-neutral names. Surnames actually. If we'd been males, our given names would've been the same. It's been a bit easier now since there are only two remaining Miss Culpeppers, Blaike and me."

None of this was any of his business.

"Perhaps you're acquainted with one or more of the lords?" A less than subtle reminder about who he was dealing with.

Something more sinister than amusement or inquisitiveness lurked in his gaze as he answered Blaike's question. "Alas, I have never had the privilege of meeting their lordships. Though I do occasionally call upon my . . . um, grandmother . . ." His intense gaze shifted to the right the merest bit, and he made a nonchalant gesture. "The Dowager Duchess of . . . ah, Brantham when I'm in England."

The Duchess of where?

Sounded like a breed of cattle or type of chicken.

Plus, he seemed rather hard put to recall his own grandmother's name.

"I would consider it the highest honor to assist two damsels far from our homeland." Captain Abraham delivered another engaging smile while surveying the dock once more.

Whatever was he looking for?

Apparently satisfied, he drew his attention back to Blaike and Blaire. "Please, forgive my boldness, but I've never seen lovelier twins. You resemble angels or goddesses with your splendid hair."

Much, *much* too forward.

Besides, given the five Culpeppers all possessed the same fairy-like shade of hair, they'd heard that pretty praise far too often for it to turn their heads.

His compliment received thin smiles. Nothing more.

Time to thank Captain Abraham and send the tenacious fellow on his way. Something about him set Blaike's teeth on edge. Her nerves, as well. She, too, glanced around, searching for what, she didn't quite know.

Something out of the ordinary.

Or someone to rush to their aid.

No knight was going to come galloping along on his steed and rescue them. No chaperone with a heavy purse, a basket of flakey French pastries, and tickets for their passage would bustle across the wharf, hailing them. No dashing buccaneer—like the fascinating Captain Whitehouse—would sprint across the dockyard, order the captain to leave off, then escort the twins safely to their ship.

After delivering the luggage to the harbor master's doorway, Captain Abraham's men lounged against the porch posts or railing, awaiting their leader's instructions. They also repeatedly scanned the surrounding area, their postures alert, almost menacing.

It struck Blaike then.

Miscreants all, the seedy lot.

Captain Abraham held the office door open, and jutting his square chin toward the weathered gray benches arranged before the dirty, low windows, wordlessly directed his men to wait there.

To a man they nodded, yet sly grins quirked their mouths as they brazenly trailed their lewd gazes over the twins.

Blaike's nape hairs sprang upward in renewed alarm.

Reluctance hardly described the sensation bombarding her. She didn't want this man interfering in their business. Looping her arm through Blaire's, she summoned her most beguiling smile.

"You needn't waste any more of your valuable time on us, Captain Abraham. I'm sure you've much to attend to."

She extended her hand for the sack containing their food, and he somewhat reluctantly relinquished it. They might have dire need of the pouch's contents.

"We are most grateful for your assistance."

"Yes, thank you." Blaire scarcely bestowed a glance in his direction.

With a dismissive nod, Blaike practically lugged Blaire into the dim office, refusing to look over her shoulder to see if Captain Abraham still stood in the entrance. From the flesh rippling up and down her spine—and across her bum, too—she'd bet on it.

"I feel like spiders are skittering over my behind," Blaire whispered. "He gives me the—"

"Shivers. Me too," Blaike acknowledged as her eyes adjusted to the darker interior. Why hadn't a lamp or a taper been lit, for pity's sake? "Let's hope the harbor master speaks English."

A wiry little fellow with the most elaborately curled and waxed mustache she'd ever seen, opened his eyes and yawned as he unhurriedly angled his booted feet to the floor.

Well, that explained the shadowy office. He'd been napping. Quite deeply too from the befuddled gaze he turned upon them.

After cutting the doorway a swift glance, and tipping his head the slightest bit—at the captain?—he sauntered to the counter.

Heavens.

Up close, the hair topping his upper lip was even more . . . astonishing. Blaike could scarcely wrench her focus from his ghastly whiskers as she placed the food atop the scarred counter. A full six inches or more extended to either side of his thin-lipped mouth, transfixing her in a grotesque way. Like an oddity at Bullock's Museum of Natural Curiosities that repulsed and mesmerized simultaneously.

However did he manage to eat or drink with that . . . *appendage*?

A sudden vision of a dainty china teacup hanging from each ornate curl, followed at once by another image of the thickly waxed strands swaying about like tentacles sprang to mind, and only by sheer force of will did she keep from laughing.

She drew her focus away for a moment to collect herself lest her trembling lips expose her struggle. Lips sucked in and eyelids cast downward, Blaire fussed with her hatbox straps, evidently as overcome with humor as Blaike.

The harbor master rested his forearms atop the

scuffed wooden surface, his lips bent into a tolerant smile. Or perhaps insolent better described his curving mouth.

"Comment puis-je vous aider mesdames?"

"Yes, please. *Oui, s'il vous plaît.*" Blaire set her hatboxes on the countertop.

That was about the extent of Blaike's French as well.

"Do you speak English? Anglais?" she asked.

"J'ai bien peur que non." Giving a rueful smile, he shook his head. His stiff mustache didn't move a jot.

"Of course he doesn't," Blaike muttered, exhaustion, hunger, and worry rendering her short on patience and politesse. Shouldn't a port captain be multi-lingual?

She met Blaire's fretful gaze.

No help for it.

They would have to impose upon Captain Abraham after all. Blaike half turned toward the door.

"Captain, I fear we must inconvenience you once again."

A prudent woman heeds this truth: a gossamer
fine thread separates listening to gossip and listening
to a secret. Make sure you know the difference.
~Scruples and Scandals
The Genteel Lady's Guide to Practical Living

3

An I-told-you-so, just this side of gloating smile curved Captain Abraham's mouth; he'd already strode halfway across the scratched floor in need of a good sweep.

"What is it you need to inquire of Monsieur Meunier, Miss Culpepper?"

"Please ask him what vessel the Culpeppers' passage to London has been arranged on." Blaike's stomach took the opportunity to announce its dissatisfaction by rumbling loudly.

Blaire sent her a compassionate glance.

However, the captain didn't flinch. Perhaps he hadn't heard or he was playing the gentleman, for which she was grateful. He rattled off her question, and a swift discourse took place between him and the agent.

Monsieur Meunier rifled through a couple of piles of papers on his desk, then the stacks behind the high counter. Every now and again, he posed another question to Captain Abraham before murmuring to himself, shaking his head, and inspecting more files.

His attention frequently slid to Blaike and her sister.

At last, he placed his palms atop the counter, and his expression apologetic, shrugged his thin shoulders. "*Je ne trouve rien sur ton transport.*"

The captain removed his hat and scraped his fingers through his curly dark brown hair, the ruby in his ring, glowing blood red in the dim office. "Are you positive passage was reserved for you, ladies? Meunier cannot find any correspondence or payment confirmation."

Speechless for an instant, Blaike stood on her toes and scrutinized the disorderly mounds on the other side of the counter. "He must be mistaken. Our sister wrote and assured us everything had been arranged."

Sympathy softening the angles of his face, Captain Abraham shook his head. "He's not. If Meunier says there's no passage booked for you, then there's not."

"Blaike, what are we to do? How are we to get home?"

Blaire didn't normally panic, but she knew full well what their circumstances were. It would take weeks for the mail ship to deliver another letter and then bring them a response.

What were they to do in the meanwhile? Where would they live? How would they eat?

Captain Abraham smiled kindly, almost in a fatherly way. Yet, within the depths of his artic eyes, Blaike glimpsed a trace of cunning. Not a man to trust despite his helpful overtures.

"No need to fret, Miss Culpepper. Providence has smiled upon you." He winked and returned his hat to his head. "As it happens, I have room for two passengers on my vessel. You'll have to share a stateroom, of course."

Either they stay stranded in *Port de Lyon* for weeks without sufficient funds or board the *Black Dove* and risk whatever might befall them under the captain's watch.

The choice was akin to asking Blaike to choose between death by fire or by water. Clearly Blaire didn't favor the captain's offer either. True aversion glinted in her troubled gaze.

As frightening as trying to find accommodations and the means to support themselves was, the other consideration cramped Blaike's lungs and dampened her palms in dread. There was something to be said about women's intuition, and hers fairly screamed, *Refuse his offer.*

He pivoted to glance out the dusty window, his shrewd-eyed gaze darting here and there.

Certainly a suspicious sort, wasn't he?

Honest men weren't this paranoid or edgy. More confirmation they should depart his company at once despite their grim situation.

Blaire gave the briefest negative shake of her head before he turned around again.

An elbow resting upon the countertop, the captain raised a calloused finger toward Blaike and her sister as he said something to Monsieur Meunier in what sounded like Spanish. For certain it wasn't French.

The harbor master fingered his gaudy mustache, his gaze swinging between Blaike and Blaire before he at last gave a slow nod. "*Oui.*"

Didn't they know it was rude to discuss people in another language? And why Spanish and not French? All the more reason to bid the captain *adieu*.

"That's most generous of you, Captain. However, the plain truth is, we haven't funds to purchase tickets. They were to have been prepaid for us."

Monsieur Meunier wouldn't meet her eyes, and she narrowed hers.

Was the scoundrel lying? But why?

And about what, exactly?

It did no good to insist on examining his documents

either, since she read French even less skillfully than she spoke the language. That shortcoming had irritated Madame Beaulieu no end.

How she'd railed at the twins, calling them *bête comme les pieds.*

Stupid as one's feet.

Why, because they didn't speak another language and hadn't become fluent in French while in Geneva? There'd been no need to read and speak French at Esherton Green, the dairy farm that had been their home until a few months ago before their cousin, Brooke married Lord Ravensdale.

Captain Abraham lifted a thick shoulder, then bold as brass, chucked Blaike's chin.

She inhaled abruptly and retreated a step.

Monsieur Meunier gave a high-pitched feminine giggle, and she lashed him a chiding glance.

"You are related to three lords, ladies. Naturally, I shall suspend payment until we arrive in London." Captain Abraham extended an arm toward the doorway. "Come, you're tired and given your stomach's growling, hungry, too. Permit me to escort you to my ship. I can even arrange hot baths for you."

The notion of being naked within a mile of him sucked every drop of moisture from Blaike's mouth.

Blaire's also, it seemed, for she swallowed audibly,

and pale as alabaster, retrieved her boxes.

Too blasted bad they'd never learned to shoot a gun, for the small unloaded pistol purchased as a gift for Blythe and tucked into one of the hatboxes might've been of some actual use about now. For certain Blaike would demand lessons once back in England.

Blaire's teasing about fencing and boxing lessons rather appealed too. Women should be permitted ways to defend themselves every bit as much as men.

The thumping of heavy feet announced new arrivals. Blaike grasped the sack of food and cast a disinterested glance toward the entrance. What she saw plummeted her heart to the scruffy floor boards.

Captain Abraham's men had entered, and the expressions on their faces confirmed her burgeoning fears.

His good-natured mien evaporated, sharpening the lean planes of his face as he edged closer, and an ominous shroud of trepidation descended upon her.

"Captain, don't force me to become rude. We've declined your offer." She grasped Blaire's elbow. "Now step aside. We're not boarding your ship."

All pretense of civility gone, he seized Blaike's upper arm in a crushing grip.

"Alas, I must insist otherwise."

Incensed over the news Oliver had just received, he and his wiry second-in-command, Jack Hawkins, strode across the wharf, anger resounding in every click of Oliver's boot heels upon the dock's coarse wood. He needed a dram or two, mayhap an entire bottle of brandy to take the edge off his fury.

This afternoon, two brokers in Lyon had reneged on shipping their cargo with him.

Spineless poltroons.

Oliver hadn't been pleased when the twitchy silk merchant dressed like a damned canary stammered his feeble excuse, all the while mopping his chubby face with his handkerchief and darting fearful glances right and left. But when the winemaker babbled the same contrived reason for breaking their contract after years of satisfactory business association—his blood had boiled.

Someone was set on systematically sabotaging and defaming him. Someone who also kept telling merchants Oliver's name was Oliviero de Casabianca.

True, de Casabianca meant Whitehouse, and *Nonno* had changed their surname to the English equivalent when he and *Mamma* had immigrated to England, over forty years ago now. Oliver assumed his grandfather had done so because he'd wanted to blend into the new country he called home. Nevertheless, Oliver's given name had never been Oliviero, so someone was deliberately spreading that lie.

Someone who'd taken the time to learn of his Italian heritage.

Every sign pointed straight to Landon Abraham, the cockscum.

If Oliver owned a pirate's treasure, he'd bet every last gold coin and glittering gemstone that the *Black Dove*'s captain had been besmirching his reputation and integrity once again. Third port just this past year, and the feeble tale was always the same. This targeting wasn't new. Far from it. Abraham had beleaguered him for years; their mutual hatred had led to an ongoing feud.

Too bad he hadn't succeeded in ending the sod's life those many years ago. God knows, he'd tried. But a small-for-his-age skinny lad had been no match for the strapping sailor who'd set fire to *Nonno's* shipping office, also burning their living quarters above. At the time, Oliver hadn't known Abraham's name, and so the cur evaded punishment for murdering *Nonno*.

At thirteen Oliver had found himself a homeless orphan.

Well, not exactly.

A muscle jumped in his jaw, he clamped his teeth so hard.

He *had* a father. George Theodore Talbot, sixth Viscount Willoughby. Willoughby owned several houses, carriages, dozens of horses, and had three legitimate offspring.

Not willing to venture down that unpleasant, too-often-trod path again, Oliver turned his thoughts to the tale he'd heard more than once since arriving in port last week.

Away on business, Monsieur Seaulieu, a wealthy textile manufacturer, had found his home torched when he returned. It seemed his daughters had rebuffed a ship captain's advances at the theater. The culprit's description matched Abraham, right down to the ruby ring on his forefinger and the scar on his face.

God how Oliver despised the cur, yet he maintained his outward composure. Inside, bitterness and contempt roiled on. He didn't need to hear another lecture on forgiveness from Hawkins at the moment, for he didn't trust himself not to tell his mate what dark abyss he could cram his well-meaning sermon into.

Hawkins didn't deserve that disrespect.

Taking a slow, deliberate breath, Oliver ordered the chaos hammering his ribs to cease.

It ignored him, as it had for years.

How he envied Hawkins's serene disposition. Oliver would never understand why the gentle soul hadn't gone into the ministry rather than taking to the sea.

He'd asked, umpteen times actually, and Hawkins always smiled and said, "God's plans are better than man's."

Whatever the blazes that meant.

Indignation roughened Hawkins's usually gentle voice as he trotted beside Oliver. "The vendors' insinuations are ludicrous, my boy."

He snorted, then spat into the dirt.

Was he actually peeved?

"Accusing you of sympathizing with Napoleon during the war. Because you're half Italian. Pure . . . pure twaddle, I say." Hawkins sounded like a prim and proper dowager or a poised spinster.

"Twaddle? Not codswallop? Balderdash? Fustian rubbish?" Despite the severity of the moment, Oliver suppressed a grin.

No matter how angry or outraged he became, his first mate did not curse. Unlike M'Lady Lottie, the vulgar-mouthed parrot Oliver had inherited last month. What that obnoxious winged termagant squawked made even his ears burn on occasion.

Hawkins's most outrageous expletive—one Oliver had only heard uttered twice in the many years they'd been acquainted—was *bleeding son of a barnacle's bum*.

Other than giving him a gimlet eye, his first mate didn't respond to the jesting. "Not only have the wars been over for years now, you were scarcely out of short pants in 1815." The older man chuckled as he hurried to keep up with Oliver's pace. "I remember well the angry, scrawny whelp who signed on as a cabin boy those many years ago."

Oliver cracked a grin then.

"And I remember well the Bible-quoting sea tar who kept lecturing me on forgiveness and controlling my temper. Oh, and honoring my father, though why you think I should is beyond me." His grin faded into a scowl. "But it still means the cargo hold won't be full, and we both know I need every contract filled to pay the crew and to make payment on the *Sea Gypsy*."

He'd already delayed payment twice. If forced to do so again, he might find himself without a ship to captain.

Then what in hellfire would he do?

"Aye, I know. But the good Lord has a reason for everything." Hawkins fell silent, a sure indication that he was petitioning the almighty on Oliver's behalf.

Right now, he'd take help from any source that offered it. Even the Almighty's, though Oliver wasn't a believer in that sort of thing. He'd seen too much and experienced too much to believe in a loving God.

The devil?

Hell, yes.

In the form of Landon Abraham.

While Oliver had captained the *Sea Gypsy* for four years, he'd contracted to purchase her last year when her owner died and his nephew, Neville Longhurst, had inherited. Truth to tell, for once, fortune had been with Oliver.

"Oliver, do you think Abraham's behind Seaulieu's house and warehouse burning?"

"Aye. I'd wager the *Sea Gypsy* on it. And I pray someone saw him this time, and he finally gets his due. Two servants died in the blaze."

Shops. Houses. Granaries. Ships.

Too many properties mysteriously went up in flames, always when Abraham was known to have been in the vicinity. Yet the *bastare* escaped justice again and again.

Probably after offering someone a sizable bribe to provide him with an alibi. How a person could be utterly corrupt to their marrow, Oliver didn't know. If Abraham ever had any redeeming qualities, he'd long since abandoned them.

Oliver wouldn't be the least surprised to learn the murmurings that Abraham had begun dabbling in smuggling and piracy were true. Smuggling, Oliver well-understood, and even he'd been tempted to accept offers to transport contraband. In the end he'd refused, not willing to risk confiscation of his ship, should he be apprehended.

A hand pressed to his temple, Oliver considered his current options. If he sailed to Bari instead of London, might he obtain additional cargo?

Perhaps, but he had no guarantee he'd be successful, and his clients waiting in England wouldn't be pleased at the delay. He couldn't afford to lose their patronage, too.

He'd rather swab the decks with his bare arse than ask his sire to speak on his behalf to his cronies. Oliver was dogged in his determination to make something of himself without accepting a pence or any form of help from Willoughby, even if the man had offered numerous times.

Offered too late to save *Mamma* or *Nonno*.

Deep in thought, Oliver marched along, glancing up after a few moments to note his whereabouts.

"Ballocks."

He'd been so absorbed in his ruminations, he'd

strode past the tavern. As he turned on his heel, something compelled him to slice a fleeting glance toward Meunier's office.

Meunier, the greasy weasel. Another miscreant deserving of retribution.

Wordlessly, Hawkins pivoted too, his lips still moving in silent entreaty to his Lord.

The port master likely knew something of this latest treachery. Swimming from Barbados to London with one's feet tied proved easier than getting that corrupt sod to confess to any underhanded dealings, however. Everyone knew he was easily bribed and often looked the other way at nefarious dealings occurring at *Port de Lyon*.

A wonder he still held his position.

Catching a glimpse of moonlit-spun hair, Oliver stumbled to an abrupt halt.

A woman of honorable character knows
full well there are people who gather secrets,
swearing to confidentiality, while all the while,
they contemplate who they'll tell first. Such are to be
avoided lest they contaminate you with their duplicity.
~*Scruples and Scandals*
The Genteel Lady's Guide to Practical Living

4

It couldn't be.

It bloody-well shouldn't be.

The Culpeppers in Lyon?

Oliver squinted, peering into the dingy window's small panes. Another equally blonde head bobbed into view for an instant.

He planted his hands on his hips, his mouth flattened into a grim line.

"Blast, damn, and devil a bit. What the hell are *they* doing here?"

"Who?" Hawkins gazed about confused, then cocked a grisly brow. Pulling his cap from his head, he scratched his bald pate. "You mean Abraham's vermin yonder? It's not the first time we've encountered that plague in port. Best to avoid them, I say. The Good Book tells us not to keep company with fools."

"No." Oliver made a disgusted sound in his throat and shook his head. "That's disturbing enough, but I fear—and I hope to your God I'm wrong—I've just spied Blaike and Blaire Culpepper in Meunier's office."

Hawkins replaced his cap while slowly rotating to face the building square on. "Burn me. That doesn't bode well. For the misses Culpepper, I mean. Think Abraham's in there with 'em?"

"I would stake my life on it. Find at least a dozen of our crew as rapidly as possible and meet me there." Hand resting on his sword hilt, Oliver canted his head in the building's direction. "Webb, Melville, and Grover just went into the *Le Savire et le Cygnet.*"

Hawkins gave a short, jerky nod. "Likely more are inside the ale house, too."

Oliver had meant to join his men in the tavern and drown his ire as he attempted to assess this latest obstacle before they weighed anchor tomorrow. "Send crewmen to ready the *Sea Gypsy* for defense and others to round the men up. We cannot weigh anchor until the tide turns, so we'd best be ready to protect her once the Culpeppers are on board. And Hawkins, say a prayer while you're at it. I have a feeling we're going to need reinforcements."

"Aye, Cap'n. Straightaway." Hitching his trousers at the waist with one hand, and grasping the crude pewter cross dangling from his neck with the other, the elf of a man set off at a brisk pace.

Oliver pivoted toward the harbor master's and, brushing his fingertips across his short beard, contemplated the situation.

Plain idiotic to approach Abraham and his thugs alone, but Blaike didn't know the danger she and her twin were in.

Abraham's alleged association with slave traders in the East put them in great peril. He'd sell the twins on the auction block, and given their unusual height, magnificent blond hair, and exquisite sapphire eyes, they'd bring a king's ransom. Abraham probably had entertained the same idea about Seaulieu's pretty honey-haired daughters.

Devil take it.

Why were the Culpeppers in Lyon?

Weren't they supposed to be at that academy for another year and a half? The last time he'd been in London, neither Ravensdale nor Leventhorpe had mentioned them returning early.

From the corner of his eye he saw a few of his men approaching, their expressions grave.

Hawkins must've apprised them of the urgency.

As long as more of Abraham's mangy crew didn't also show up, things might be settled without a major brawl or the constable intervening. Delaying the *Sea Gypsy's* departure because her crew cooled their tempers in jail meant another direct hit to Oliver's none-too-heavy purse.

If he lost the *Sea Gypsy* . . .

Giving himself a mental shake, he directed his musing to the matter at hand.

"Too much to hope the authorities might arrive and arrest Abraham for setting the fire," Oliver muttered to himself. "Regrettably, I seldom have that kind of good fortune."

"I said unhand me, you . . . you Johnny bum."

Blaike.

Despite the very real danger, his lip twitched at her depiction of a horse's arse.

Most people couldn't tell her and her twin apart, but Oliver had been able to since they first met. Her sister had a small mole by her right eyebrow that Blaike didn't. Blaike's voice was slightly huskier than her twin's, and her eyes fairly sparkled with azure mischief when she was amused.

Which was frequently.

His spirit also recognized another discontented,

driven soul, though she hid it well beneath lowered lashes and a skillfully masked expression. A people-pleaser from what he'd observed, she did her utmost to keep from distressing others.

At what cost, though?

"Ouch, you brute." A pained cry filtered through the office's open doorway.

Oliver sprinted across the wharf, half-listening for his men, and half-straining to hear Blaike or her sister. They had some explaining to do, by Jove. However, his first concern was seeing the twins safely aboard the *Sea Gypsy*. No easy task if Abraham and the barbarians he surrounded himself with were determined otherwise.

Slowing his pace, he crept onto the low porch. A board creaked, and he froze mid-step. A swift glance over his shoulder reassured him. Several of his men hurried in his direction.

The crew was the family he'd longed for since his grandfather had been murdered. Loyal and dedicated, each hand on the *Sea Gypsy* would sacrifice their life for another's.

All except for the new cook they'd taken on in Jamaica after McMaster indulged in too much mumbo and stumbled off a pier. He'd hit his head and drowned. Fairnly, his replacement, was a queer one, and he hated M'Lady Lottie as much as the bird despised him.

Oliver slowly drew his sword and peeked around the doorjamb.

Abraham held Blaike's arm in a cruel grip as she wrestled to free herself, defiance shooting from her glorious eyes.

Blaire stood statue still, terror radiating off her.

"You will either walk of your own accord, or you'll be carried, writhing and shrieking," Abraham threatened, shaking her so hard, a few tendrils slipped loose from their pins.

Blaike cried out again, and Blaire lunged forward, pulling on Abraham's forearm. The hatboxes she held tumbled to the floor. "Stop it, you evil lout! You're hurting her."

Exquisite in a rumpled Pomona green and lavender traveling gown, Blaike went rigid, arching away from him. "You—" She veered his men a panicked glance. "They would not dare. Besides, someone would come to our aid."

She trembled so hard, her jaunty little hat shook atop her shimmering hair, yet she stoically attempted to keep her composure.

"I would dare, and no fool would interfere with a concerned father disciplining his run-away daughters, right chaps?" Brow cocked, Abraham laughed, deep and sinister. Eyes glittering with malicious excitement, the whoremonger was relishing their fear.

"Aye, Cap'n. You've been plain heartsick with fear for them," Eades agreed before he and his mates guffawed, pounding each other on the back and shoulders. "Bet they smell good. Ladies always do. I wouldn't mind carrying either wench." His lewd appraisal stripped the twins bare. "Toss her over my shoulder and squeeze her plump arse as I walk."

Oliver's hand grew numb from the stranglehold he had on his sword. He shot a glance over his shoulder. Just a few more moments . . .

"No. If it comes to that, Demir will carry the other twin. I trust him not to molest her." Scowling, Abraham narrowed his eyes to slits and leveled each of his men a murderous glare. "They are to remain untouched. Do you understand? Virgins until we reach Cairo." Nostrils flared, he licked his lips. "They'll bring us a bloody fortune."

"Dear God, no." Blaire staggered backward, banging into the counter and kicking a hatbox. Revulsion drained her face of color as she pressed a hand to her throat, exchanging an horrorstruck glance with Blaike.

"Let me go, bloody blackguard." Blaike renewed her frantic struggles, several more flaxen strands tumbling to her shoulders as she jerked and tugged.

"And how can you be so certain we're virgins. We might not be."

Abraham chuckled again.

"If you aren't, then I'll sample your charms myself on the voyage and let my officers share your twin." He leaned nearer, mere inches separating his gloating face and Blaike's white-as-fresh-milk countenance. "And I'll still sell you, though unfortunately, for far less."

She swallowed, and closing her eyes, averted her face.

Deadly rage hummed through Oliver. It pounded in his ears, welled in his chest, and inflamed his blood. He wanted Abraham dead. By his hand.

Throughout it all, Meunier leaned nonchalantly against his desk, arms folded. No surprise that cawker wouldn't help two women in distress. His perverse preferences ran to young boys, often supplied by Abraham.

How many women had he abetted in trafficking, the whoremonger?

"*Naturellement*, I'll receive *mon habituel* fee?" he said.

Blaike gasped, and her eyelids flew open as she swung her infuriated gaze to him. "Spawn of Satan. You do speak English!"

"*Oui*." He shrugged, fingering his atrocity of a

mustache. "Anglais, Espanol, and bits of others."

Abraham hauled a resisting Blaike closer, his lust apparent. Only his greed would keep him from despoiling her the instant he had her aboard his ship. "I'll tend to this one myself. I have other ways she can be of use to me on the voyage."

Such scorching fury engulfed Oliver at the crude insinuation, he bit the inside of his cheek to keep from revealing his presence. Daring a last glance behind him, he twisted his mouth into a satisfied smirk.

Pistols, swords, and dirks drawn, his men advanced.

"You'll dance in hell first."

Blaike released a hoarse cry and spun to face the entrance, relief blossoming across her exquisite features.

"Captain Whitehouse! Oh, thank God. I knew Blythe had made arrangements for our passage."

Where had she come by that false notion?

If Blaike had arrived a day later, the *Sea Gypsy* would've already made the Mediterranean.

He wouldn't have been able to save them from a fate too horrific to contemplate.

Oliver, his legs spread-eagle and sword in hand, impaled Abraham with his gaze. How he longed to bury his blade in the libertine over and over. He pointed a finger toward Blaike and Blaire. "Their guardian entrusted me with the Culpeppers care on the voyage here, and I shall see them to London. Unlike you, I'll make damned sure they're returned to their family safely."

Oliver's men clambered onto the porch and into the office.

Metal scraped against metal as Abraham's men drew their weapons. They were outnumbered at least three to one, and though Abraham wasn't one to back down from a fight, he preferred to skulk round under the cover of darkness. A noisy, attention-grabbing ruckus wouldn't serve him well.

"*Tsk, tsk.*" Shaking his head, Oliver jabbed a thumb over his shoulder. "You may want to rethink your impulse, lads. Scabber your blades. Now. Better yet, drop them."

To a man, Abraham's crew shot their captain a questioning gaze.

He gave a tense jerk of his head, and muttering vulgarities, they dropped their knives and swords. The metal clanged loudly as it hit the floor.

Hawkins edged to Oliver's side. "Cap'n, everythin' is as you bid, and I've had the misses' luggage taken to the ship."

He hurried to retrieve Blaire's hatboxes, then

passed them to a deckhand.

"Excellent." Adjusting his grip on his sword, Oliver wielded the tip at Abraham. "I believe Miss Culpepper asked you to unhand her."

Abraham did so, hate curling his lip. The motion pleated the scar Oliver had given him that fateful night. "You expect me to believe *you*, uneducated gutter filth with scarcely two coins to rub together and a known by-blow, were entrusted with the Culpeppers' passage here?"

If the cur intended to shame Oliver with his revelations, he fell short of the mark. Everything he said was true and common knowledge.

Blaike stabbed Abraham with a lethal glare before she swept Oliver a pity-filled gaze. The sympathy in her shining eyes cut a gash far deeper and more painful than Abraham's spiteful words.

"Yes, he was, Captain. Because he, unlike you, is a man of integrity, despite the origins of his birth." She took her sister's hand, and they scooted past the lurking hulks. A few feet from Abraham, Blaike whirled around. "Honor and high character can raise a person above their birth and circumstances. Most especially if whatever shadows them wasn't their fault. That is why, Captain Abraham, you will always, *always,* muck about with the lowest," her attention gravitated to his men, "most vile of offensive creatures."

She marched to Oliver, ushering her trembling sister before her. "Captain Whitehouse, if you would be so kind as to escort us to the *Sea Gypsy*. I've quite enough of French hospitality for a lifetime."

White lines framed her mouth, revealing just how much effort it took to retain her composure. Most women facing the prospect of being sold into white slavery, would have dissolved into hysterics.

"Wait outside," he gently ordered, touching her arm.

Lips pursed, she gave a brief nod as she passed.

"Don't let Abraham or his brutes move until we are well away from here," Oliver instructed Hawkins. He gestured to more of his crew, then pointed at Abraham's thugs. "You make sure they don't budge, either. And search them all for other weapons."

"As you say, Cap'n." Hawkins canted his head toward Oliver's men. "Lads, check their boots, while you're at it."

As his mates rushed to further disarm Abraham and his crew, Oliver took the opportunity to corner Meunier. Once he'd sheathed his sword, Oliver grabbed the harbor master by his collar and shoved him so hard against the wall pinned with an assortment of bulletins, two fluttered to the floor.

"You'd be wise to resign your position and disappear into the gutters where your kind belongs, Meunier." Righteous outrage humming through his blood, Oliver tightened his hold. "Because I assure you, when the Culpepper Misses' family learns your part in this debacle, those powerful lords will demand retribution. You won't stand a maggot's chance in a hen yard of escaping unscathed."

Meunier's jaw hung slack, and he quivered like a fledgling leaf buffeted by a North Sea gale. His damned mustache still remained morbidly stiff, though.

"God, I hate that revolting thing." Oliver yanked his dagger from its cover, and Meunier released a strangled terrified squeak. Oliver slashed off either side of the offending atrocity, dropping the disgusting waxed strands onto the floor. "Consider that a favor. It made you look like an imbécile."

Eyes closed, a tear dribbling from the corner of one, Meunier sagged against the wall, gasping.

As Oliver returned his blade to its leather case, he grimaced. "Soiled yourself, did you? Be a good chap and light a lamp before attending to that offensiveness."

A few men snickered.

"The sod shite himself?"

"Twiddlepoop."

"Buggering Molly."

"Enough," Oliver snapped. Like hens sensing weaker chickens, the men attacked with barbed rejoinders. He'd meant to scare the hell out of Meunier and teach him a lesson—not subject him to ridicule, even if he deserved it. "Tend to your tasks."

Besides, the Culpeppers were only a few feet away and shouldn't be exposed to such course language.

As Meunier shuffled to do Oliver's bidding, Abraham attempted to follow the twins.

The *click* of Hawkins cocking his blunderbuss drew everyone's gaze.

"Abraham, I'm thinkin' you've not repented of your evil ways nor made your peace with the Good Lord. As much as it would grieve me to send any soul to burn in hell for eternity, if you move another inch, I'll blow a hole in your skull—right between your shifty devil's eyes—and ask The Almighty's forgiveness afterward."

"You don't have the ballocks, you puny little bastard," Abraham sneered, though he stopped sidling toward the entrance. "My men would run you through."

Hawkins raised the pistol, pointing the barrel squarely at Abraham's forehead, and lifted a boney shoulder. "You'd be dead, and I'd be enterin' the pearly gates. Good enough for me. Besides, they'd have to get to me, and I'm thinkin' a lead ball would find a home in each of their ugly faces before they moved a foot. Cannot help but think it'd be an improvement in their ugly appearances."

Hands fisted, his face contorted in frustration, Abraham swiveled to face Oliver. "We will meet again, Whitehouse, and next time, I promise you, I'll not be as amiable."

This is amiable?

Oliver chuckled. "I'll look forward to it."

Dusk had settled on Lyon, and with it, the cold that early spring evenings bring. His stomach growled, reminding him he hadn't eaten since disembarking the *Sea Gypsy* this morning.

He actually looked forward to the journey home now—a vast change from a mere hour ago.

The blonde beauty waiting outside could be credited for that.

More commotion drew Oliver's attention outdoors. Flanked on either side by columns of soldiers, the first two carrying lanterns, an important-looking man and what Oliver presumed was the constable made straight for the Harbor Master's Office.

Well, now. Mayhap Abraham was about to get his comeuppance after all.

Oliver raised a brow and rubbed his beard as he angled Abraham a considering glance. "I'm fairly certain that gentleman is Seaulieu. Wonder what brings him here? He looks to be in a fine fettle, too."

"Hell and damnation," Abraham mumbled, shifting toward the window. "Meunier, is there another way out?"

Meunier had disappeared into a back room.

"*Ah, ah, ah.*" Hawkins clicked his tongue. "I warned you not to move an inch. And keep your hands where I can see them, you scurvy sea-dog. You wouldn't want me to pull the trigger when all you were doin' was satisfyin' an indelicate itch, now would you?"

Oliver bent into a mocking bow. "I'll say my farewells. Far too many soldiers approach to fit comfortably in here. I confess, if I wasn't keen to see the Misses Culpepper to my ship, I'd linger to watch the outcome."

"Sod off, Whitehouse." Abraham spared Oliver a sneering glower before he returned his rapt attention to the window and the advancing soldiers.

"Hawkins," Oliver said, "I'll see you aboard ship."

"Aye, Cap'n." He grinned and sliced a quick glance heavenward. "Looks like the Good Lord heard my prayer 'bout reinforcements."

"Indeed."

Pleased to have bested Abraham this round, Oliver stalked onto the porch. Those of his men not inside the office or on his ship loitered nearby, each alert and ready to jump into action should the need arise. To a man, they watched the soldiers' progression, their weather-browned faces curious.

Blaike and her sister rested on a time-worn bench, arms around one another's waists. Shoulders hunched and gazes wary, weariness blanketed them. He couldn't venture to guess what had brought them to Lyon, but he'd be bound it wasn't anything good.

He might not have a full cargo hold, but he'd have the pleasure of Blaike's company on the voyage home. Not a bad trade-off at all. Actually, it would be a pleasurable hell, having her near once more and never being able to declare himself.

Still, he'd take the treasured gift.

Her soft mouth turned up into a tired, fragile smile at his approach, then suddenly her eyes became huge and terrified, and she lurched to her feet, pointing.

"Oliver! Behind you!"

Eyes often reveal the secrets of
one's heart, and an astute woman will
watch to see if they confirm what is spoken.
~Scruples and Scandals
The Genteel Lady's Guide to Practical Living

5

B laike dashed into the captain's shadowy quarters, holding a lantern before her.

"Hairy-lipped trollop!"

Giving a startled yelp, she spun toward the grating voice.

Its salmon-crested head cocked to the side, a white bird sat atop a perch inside a cage. An odd assortment of things hung inside, including silverware tied together, ropes, wood pieces, colorful beads, rings, and a mirror. Beside the cage stood a sturdy perch made from a branch. It, too, had several items dangling from it.

Must be toys.

Why did it surprise her that Oliver had a pet bird?

Was it new, for surely Blaike would've heard its screeching on the previous voyage?

Why couldn't he have a normal pet like her cats, Pudding and Dumpling, or dear toddling half-blind, mostly-deaf old Freddy, their Welsh corgi?"

"Hello luv." The bird flapped its wings, revealing subtle yellow on its underwings.

"Hello to you, too." *Rude little beast.* "Your master's been hurt."

After setting the lantern aside, Blaike untied her bonnet and tossed the dainty hat and her reticule onto an impressive desk covered with charts and an assortment of interesting looking nautical tools, as well as an hourglass, quill, and an unusual bronze ship shaped inkwell.

What were the instruments used for?

A few detailed, excellent sketches of sailing vessels lay upon the desktop as well, and several more adorned the great cabin's walls. Had he drawn them? She was no expert at such things, but even she could recognize immense talent when she saw it.

Her attention drifted back to the curious gadgets.

Mayhap when he recovered, she might ask Oliver to show her how to use them. She'd always been interested in ship's navigation.

On the voyage from London, she hadn't been inside his cabin, and now amid a crisis, she was intrigued about the contents?

Had she known what Geneva held for her, she'd never have set foot on the *Sea Gypsy* last autumn, and Oliver wouldn't be bleeding all over the floor right now.

Twisting her mouth, she eyed the dark stain marring her spencer. Ruined for certain.

"I want out. I want out," the bird demanded.

And have it flying about as Blaike tended Oliver?

Not a chance.

Besides, how did she know it was friendly? That beak looked positively dangerous.

'No, you may not come out right now." Did the creature understand? Didn't birds just mimic words and sounds?

"Curse ye, cockscum."

Good heavens.

Was there ever such a foul-mouthed creature that wasn't human? She sent Oliver a castigating glance. Just where had the beast acquired his or her vocabulary from?

No time for that now.

Oliver had been shot.

He groaned, opened his eyes again for an instant, then the lids fluttered shut once more.

Several times on the way to the ship, he'd done the same, even uttering a low oath more than once. He'd suffered a blow to his head when he collapsed, and that had frightened her as much as the ball to his shoulder.

The wound didn't appear fatal, but then, what did Blaike know of such things?

Swiftly scanning the chamber, she spied a Turkish towel draped over a washstand. She grabbed it, another smaller cloth, and the plain white porcelain basin, then rushed to spread the towel upon the rich maroon, nut brown, and beige counterpane spread atop the bed dominating the stateroom.

"Quickly, put the captain on the bed, and one of you light the lamps in here. It's far too dark to assess his injuries."

"Hell's ballocks and bells," the bird squawked.

Two burly seaman, their faces creased with worry, carefully helped their captain to his bed.

Bobbing up and down, the bird yelled, "Bugger yourself."

"Beg your pardon for that," the younger sailor said, canting his head toward the foul-mouthed fowl, his face flushed red as the scarf tied around his neck.

"What kind of bird is it?" After unfastening her spencer, Blaike slid the jacket off, letting it drop to the floor. She toed it aside. Blood marred her gown across her bosoms as well. At least she didn't have to worry about covering the garment whilst she treated Oliver.

"A Moluccan cockatoo," the older seaman offered

as he went about lighting the lamps attached to the walls and the one atop the desk.

"Do you have a surgeon on board, Mister . . .?" Blaike raised her head after checking Oliver's neck for a pulse. It beat sure and strong beneath her fingertips. "Forgive me, but I don't know your names."

"I'm Tom Grover, the quartermaster," the stocky red-head in his fifth decade said. "And this here is Jimmy Webb, our bosun's mate."

The younger, somber-faced fellow didn't look to be much older than Blaike. Yet from his serious expression and even more solemn eyes, she guessed he'd not had an easy time of it.

"Is anyone on the ship medically trained?" Blaike shoved a curl behind her ear.

His face pinched with anxiety, Mr. Webb shook his head. "No, miss. Our other cook used to take care of those things, but Fairnly's new. He ain't never treated our crew yet, and I don't know if he has the know-how McMaster did 'bout medicine."

Goose butt feathers. It just figures.

She pulled Oliver's unlaced crimson shirt farther apart, trying not to stare at the manly display of crisp, black chest hair. She lifted hers and Blaire's reddened handkerchiefs from his wounded right shoulder. After dropping them into the basin, she folded the smaller square and pressed it to his injury.

That much she remembered.

Pressure to stop the bleeding.

She closed her eyes, summoning up every recollection she could of times at Esherton Green when a person or a creature had been injured.

There weren't a whole lot, truth be told.

"Move yer fat arse," the cockatoo shrieked, and Blaike jumped.

"Can one of you possibly take the captain's pet somewhere else?"

"*Umm*, she ain't exactly friendly." Mr. Webb eyed the cage. "There's a larger cage on the poop deck, but Cap'n Whitehouse doesn't like M'Lady Lottie above deck while we weigh or drop anchor."

"Drop anchor 'twixt yer thighs," she squawked, flapping her wings.

"M'Lady?" Blaike arced her brows in disbelief even as heat scorched her cheeks. "With that vulgar vocabulary? Surely you jest."

"McMaster was raised in a whor— Um . . . that is, his mother was a—"

"Cook," Mr. Grover hastily offered. "Mrs. McMaster was one fine *cook*."

"Aye, yes. A . . . a cook. In a broth—house of ill-repute. McMaster must've learned his extraordinary skills from her," Mr. Webb stammered.

Mr. Grover made a peculiar choking sound and frantically shook his head.

"Cooking, I mean. She taught McMaster how to cook. Not to . . ." Mr. Webb colored redder than Oliver's shirt but forged on. "M'Lady was his as a boy, and now that he's died, she won't eat much for anyone but the cap'n. Grieving, he says. We think she's about twenty years old."

Wonderful. Almost two decades to learn curses, vulgarities, and insults from strumpets and sailors. And whoever heard of a ship's cook also being the medical officer? Was the ability to wield a butcher knife the only qualification to appointment as a ship's medical officer?

"What's yer pleasure?" M'Lady Lottie asked, hanging upside down.

"I suppose that means she must stay." Blaike sighed and shook her head. "Can you at least cover her cage?" She pulled a quilt from the foot of the bed. "Here, use this."

Perhaps the bird would cease her obnoxious chattering.

Mr. Webb hurried to do as bid

"Bloody whoremonger," M'Lady Lottie screamed as the quilt descended, then in a softer, plaintive voice called, "Petey? Petey?"

"That was McMaster's given name," Mr. Grover volunteered, his worried gaze trained on Oliver.

What would happen to M'Lady Lottie if Oliver too—

No. He would be fine. He must.

"I shall need hot water, clean cloths, long strips for a bandages—a cut up sheet will suffice." *What else?* "Salve if you have it, whisky, and . . ."

"Stop fussing over me," Oliver grumbled.

"Shush, and save your strength." Raising the cloth a fraction, she bent over him and examined the wound again.

A vague aroma wafted upward from his bronzed skin. Fresh, yet slightly musky, too. Maybe even a hint of cinnamon, cloves, and coffee. Most tantalizing.

Did he go shirtless when at sea? The notion caused an interesting quiver in her belly.

And utterly ridiculous that she'd notice at a time like this.

Glancing upward, her attention caught on the beard covering his olive-toned jaw. He was the only man she knew who sported facial hair, and she found it quite suave, as she did his dark coloring.

Was his beard soft or scratchy?

Enough ogling the unconscious man. For pity's sake, Blaike Regina Lillian Culpepper.

"Petey?" Pitiful and heartbroken this time. After a bit of shuffling around and feather ruffling, M'Lady Lottie fell silent.

Blaike scrutinized Oliver's injury again. Not really a hole, but more of a long furrow.

Did he need stitches?

Should they send for a surgeon? A physician?

How was she to know?

She'd never doctored anyone before. Blythe had always tended the sick and wounded.

If a physician were summoned, might that delay the ship's departure? Somehow she knew that would infuriate Oliver. It was worth the risk if doing so saved his life, however.

Did Blaike have the stomach to suture the wound?

Gads.

She swallowed, her attention drawn to his striking face.

Yes, if she must.

Her disgruntled empty tummy took the opportunity to churn sickeningly and momentary light-headedness engulfed her. Taking measured breaths, she willed the dizziness to go away. It didn't help that she was so famished, her navel gnawed at her backbone.

She glanced at the sailors, then blew out a sigh. "At least fetch the other supplies, Mr. Grover, at once, if you please. Your captain bled quite a lot on the way to the ship."

Not to mention the blood he'd lost while transferring him below deck, as their stained clothing testified.

Blaire had nearly swooned at the sight of so much blood: one of the few differences between the twins. Blaike possessed a stronger constitution, and unlike Blaire, didn't suffer from *mal de mer* either.

Poor Blaire.

If this was like the first crossing, Blaire would spend the first three days curled into a miserable ball in her berth, yet she hadn't said one word of protest about the return voyage by sea. Prior to leaving the academy, they'd discussed traveling by land most of the way home, but Blythe hadn't known that.

"Aye, miss. We'll get what you need." Mr. Grover slanted another troubled glance at his captain.

"Can you also look in on my sister, and if possible, see that she has a bite to eat?" Hopefully, he'd change his clothing first, else he might be picking Blaire off of her stateroom floor.

"Of course, Miss. I'll ask for tea as well," Mr. Webb offered.

Blaike rolled up her sleeves, then attempted to pin her drooping hair. "Tell her I'll be along as quickly as I can. She doesn't handle blood well, else she'd also help." A smile tugged her mouth upward. "Better to let her have a lie down rather than risk her swooning and getting knocked in the head, too."

They'd barely reached the door when a sharp rap preceded Hawkins rushing into the cabin as if chased by the devil himself. He pulled up short upon seeing Mr. Grover and Mr. Webb.

"What are you still doin' here?" A note of fear crept into Mr. Hawkins's voice and the look he hurled Oliver bordered on panic.

His countenance grave, Mr. Webb rubbed his furrowed forehead. "We just now got the cap'n to his chamber, sir."

Given the profuse, under-their-breath swearing coming from all three men, it'd been no easy task.

"And we're about to fetch medical supplies for Miss Culpepper to tend him," he said.

"Off with you then, and no dallyin'." Hawkins swept his cap from his head and then stuffed it into his waistband.

"Aye, sir," chorused Grover and Webb as they hurried from the captain's quarters.

"For the love of God, stop blathering and be gone." Oliver was not a compliant patient.

M'Lady Lottie stirred. She made soft, throaty

noises and ruffled her feathers, but hurled no ear-burning phrases.

"How is he?" Hawkins asked without preamble, giving the quilt atop the birdcage an inquisitive glance.

Eyes closed, Oliver mumbled, "I'm fine."

Blaike exchanged a knowing glance with Mr. Hawkins and lifted a shoulder.

"I'm honestly not sure. I don't know if the captain needs his wound sewn. I've no experience with serious injuries. He hit his head when he fell, but it's not bleeding. He woke almost immediately, but other than cursing a bit, hasn't said much. He does have quite a bump though, near a scar along his hairline. I think those are his only injuries."

"I'm capable of explaining my own condition, Miss Culpepper."

"Don't be so crotchety to the lass," Hawkins admonished as he rushed to his master's bed. *Tsking* and *tutting,* he examined Oliver's head and then the gash.

"Leave off, Hawkins." Oliver flinched and turned his head away.

"Good thing you're such a stubborn, hard-headed fool. Just a nasty lump that'll give you a whale of a headache. Your shoulder is barely scratched, thanks to Miss Culpepper's warnin'."

That was a scratch?

She offered a tremulous smile. "I wasn't quick enough. Monsieur Meunier still managed to shoot Captain Whitehouse."

"Just a glancin' blow. Hardly a nick at all," Hawkins assured her, though worry creased his brow and pulled his silver-whiskered jaw downward.

Who was he trying to reassure?

Blaike or himself?

Oliver groaned again, and his thick-lashed eyelids fluttered open. Pain had darkened his eyes to coal-black, and he shut his lids again. He swallowed audibly, his Adam's apple bobbing up and down the strong column of his thick throat, then he licked his lips.

Blaike glanced around for something to wet his mouth.

"Do you have anything in your cabin to drink?" she asked.

"Brandy. Bottom left desk drawer," he managed, his voice gruff. Wincing, he raised his left hand and touched the side of his head, whispering through his strong, white teeth, "Ho-ly hell."

"Ho-ly hell," M'Lady Lottie repeated in a raucous sing-song voice. "Ho-ly hell. Holy hell. Hoolee—"

"M'Lady Lottie, hush," Oliver ordered, squinting at the cage. "Go to sleep."

In response, the parrot screeched, "Lift yer skirts."

"Charming." Blaike couldn't have prevented her blush or her brows from climbing up her forehead if forbidden figgy pudding—she adored figgy pudding—for life.

"Need to teach her new phrases, my boy. Scriptures, poetry, nursery rhymes," Hawkins advised, his pointed ears glowing tulip red. He bustled to the desk and momentarily retrieved a bottle and three small tumblers. He raised a glass. "Miss Culpepper?"

"Thank you, no." The few instances when she'd sampled anything stronger than wine or ratafia, she'd found the flavor much too bold.

Oliver attempted to sit up, but she gently yet firmly, pressed him back into the pillows. "You're injured, and until we know how badly, you cannot be moving around."

Dark brows pulled together in a fierce scowl, he reminded her of a surly boy denied his way.

"I cannot be lazing about. I have a ship to captain, and we sail on the tide." Voice stronger than a moment ago, Oliver raised his head again. His dull eyes and the stark angles of his face exposed the discomfort he strove to mask with curt bravado. "Hawkins, my brandy, if you please."

"Aye, Cap'n." A grin twitching his mouth, Mr. Hawkins dutifully brought Oliver his spirits.

Face pale as the pillows cradling his dark head, Oliver pulled his handsome mouth into a taut line and scooted into a sitting position, his movements slow and precise.

"You really shouldn't, Oliver. You'll bleed all over your bed." Blaike rushed to prop pillows behind him as he accepted the brandy from his mate, then tossed it back in one gulp.

"More." He extended the glass, his belly gurgling loud and long.

"Most assuredly not. Especially since I gather from your rumbling stomach, you're hungry, too." Blaike took the tumbler, pointedly ignoring the sudden irritated slashing together of his brows once more. "I know you're in pain, but head injuries can be serious. We must make sure you aren't concussed. Now please, do lie back."

Oliver sighed but complied. Turning a sharp eye on Mr. Hawkins, he asked, "Is everyone aboard? The cargos are loaded, and she's ready to weigh anchor? Are guards stationed as a precaution?"

"Aye, Cap'n, to all." Mr. Hawkins nodded and finished his brandy as well. "I'll go up top and oversee the final preparations. I'll also request a tray for you." He opened the door, and after stepping through the entrance, poked his head back in for a second. "Grover's comin' with the supplies you asked for, Miss Culpepper."

"Oliver, stay put." Blaike pointed her forefinger, giving him her starchiest do-not-test-me look.

Other than closing his eyes and grimacing, he didn't respond.

Most assuredly not a good-natured patient.

With an appreciative smile, she accepted the basket from Mr. Grover. "Thank you."

"I also brought you a medicine chest and a book I found about doctoring that you might find useful." He set both on the desk.

Still not sure how to best treat Oliver, she mentally cataloged the items in the basket. "How is my sister?"

"She's settling into your stateroom, Miss. I've asked that a tray be taken to her, as well." Mr. Grover kept peering past Blaike, worry scrunching his rugged features. He slanted his gaze toward Oliver. "Has he awoken yet?"

"Yes, I have." Material shifted and crackled with Oliver's strained movements, and Blaike whirled to confront him. Slightly hunched, he sat on the edge of the bed, his face wan and a wide palm pressed to the cloth covering his wound.

"Don't you dare stand up, Oliver Whitehouse!" Her voice rang shriller than she'd intended, but ashen and unstable as he was, she feared he'd topple onto the planking.

"I think you're forgetting who gives the orders on this vessel, Miss Culpepper."

Some claim those who keep secrets are wise, but 'tis far more prudent to have no secrets worth keeping, much less confidences one dreads having revealed.

~Scruples and Scandals
The Genteel Lady's Guide to Practical Living

6

"There's little chance of that, you codpated buffoon," Blaike retorted.

Going all stubborn and bullish now, was Oliver?

Did he think to intimidate her?

Compared to Madame Beaulieu, he was nothing but a scratching, hissing kitten.

One of his raven brows vaulted ceilingward as he gingerly lifted the reddened square and examined his wound. He gave a contemptuous snort. "I've seen worse flea bites."

Bent on being uncooperative, *hmm*?

Upon spying a small brown bottle in the basket, she tilted her mouth upward into a tiny half-smile.

Laudanum.

Lovely, lovely laudanum.

That changed things a mite, indeed it did. She had just the means to keep him in his surprisingly big bed if he wanted to act the obstinate boor.

"This ship needs a captain, as you yourself reminded me not five minutes ago." She rummaged in the basket a bit more.

Tweezers. Scissors. Needles.

She shuddered the merest bit as trepidation scampered across her shoulders.

Let's hope it doesn't come to that.

"If you injure yourself further, how are we to depart?" Giving him an acrid gaze, she looped the basket onto her arm and marched to the bed.

His expression bordered on exasperated as he snapped, "My crew is perfectly capable of sailing the *Sea Gypsy*."

Ah, good to know. Just in case the laudanum was required after all. To subdue a certain mulish captain.

"I don't doubt that in the least. Remember, I've voyaged with you before." And had covertly watched him like the smitten school girl she was the entire voyage. Head tilted and mouth pursed, Blaike cupped a hip with one hand.

She sent Mr. Grover a sidelong glance. "Is he usually this cantankerous when indisposed?"

"No, Miss. He's always this belligerent." Mr.

Grover chuckled, his sage green eyes lighting with humor.

"Stow it, Grover," Oliver practically growled.

Mr. Grover, his eyes twinkling, winked at Blaike. "I should think he'd spare you some leeway since you threw yourself atop him to protect him after he'd been shot."

He'd seen that, had he?

She could feel Oliver's intense scrutiny, drat Mr. Grover.

Blaike busied herself with the medicines to hide the flush sweeping her face.

Oliver turned an annoyed gaze to his man. "It's just a flesh wound. Get yourself topside and help Hawkins. I don't need another nursemaid hovering over me blathering nonsense. Keep a sharp eye out for any sign of trouble."

After delivering a two-fingered salute, Mr. Grover took his leave, still grinning.

He must've concluded the same thing Blaike had.

Anyone as pigheaded and sour-tempered as Oliver wasn't going to cock up his toes any time soon.

She plopped the basket beside his black leather clad thighs.

"I for one don't wish to tempt Fate any further. We're fortunate Abraham and Meunier were detained by the authorities, but I'd rather not linger in port." She lifted the cloths for bandages, then set them aside.

"They were?" That news brought a bit of color to Oliver's pale cheeks, and he straightened. "'Bout time."

A rolled bandage in one hand, she nodded.

"Yes, and those three fierce buffoons with him, too. I hate to think what would've happened if they hadn't already been unarmed. As it was, it took four men to subdue each of them. I'm quite certain one soldier had a broken arm and another a shattered nose before the kerfuffle was over."

"Most likely Abraham will bribe his way out, if not within hours, then days." Disgust riddled Oliver's voice, and his expression turned rather fierce. He slapped his left knee. "Blast, but I loathe corrupt officials and those in influential positions abusing their power."

He searched her face, his anger replaced by concern. "I truly regret that you and your sister endured any of this."

Blaike set the bandage aside, still shaken by the recollection of the violence she'd witnessed but an hour ago. More so by the gun pointed at Oliver's head. If he hadn't ducked and hit Meunier's hand when he spun around . . .

"Did you really protect me?" Voice husky, it almost seemed like he was asking something more. "Is that why your gown is stained with blood? You're not injured?"

"Yes, to the first two questions, and no to the latter."

Instinct.

That was all it had been.

She'd have done the same for anyone.

Wouldn't she have?

As she'd shielded Oliver, trying to stop the bleeding, she had looked on in renewed terror as Abraham and his crew fought the soldiers and Oliver's men. Never had she witnessed such ferocity and savagery.

"One of your hands tackled Meunier as he tried to run from the fray. I think his name is Melville. He showed great restraint, given Meunier had just attempted to murder you. I believe there are others in your crew who would've killed him without a qualm."

She'd rather have liked to club the port master upside his pasty head.

"I deserved to be shot."

"I beg your pardon?"

Tweezers in hand, Blaike blinked in disbelief.

"Why would you say such a ludicrous thing? Of course you didn't. You, Oliver, rescued us from a fate so utterly vile, I can scarce think on it without trembling. He would've let Blaire and I be sold into slavery. I have little compassion for the worm of a man."

"Yes, he's a maggot. A contemptuous blot on humanity. But I humiliated him." Oliver starred across the stateroom, his jaw tense. "I know too well what it's like to be belittled. I should've handled it differently."

Blaike didn't know what to say.

She didn't agree in the least, but suspected something more than his threatening Meunier was at work here.

Holding his right arm against his torso, he sighed and closed his eyes, the lashes dark fans upon his high cheekbones.

"I'm no better than Abraham."

"Now that's absolute rubbish. You'd never have sold my sister and me, would you have?"

Icy fear zipped from her neck to her waist when he didn't respond. She touched his face. "Oliver?"

He opened those incredibly dark eyes, and for an instant, she was lost in their depths—a connection she couldn't put words to holding her fast and quickening her pulse.

It had been thus since they'd first met.

Did he feel it too?

"Blaike." He grazed his fingertips along her jaw, his voice velvety and deep. "Why are you in Lyon?"

The warmth that held her entranced evaporated,

replaced by shame and disquiet. She couldn't tell him. Couldn't bear to see either pity or accusation in his eyes because of her stupidity.

"Come, Oliver. We must see your shirt off you before the blood dries any more than it already has. Lift your good arm, and I think I can manage to work it down your other. The shirt is beyond saving, I fear."

Not a minute passed before she regretted her decision. If she thought it was hard to be this close to him, touching him with his blood-soaked shirt, seeing him shirtless, all manly bulges and sculpted muscles . . .

If she were the sort to swoon, she'd feel faint, for certain. Only, the feelings cavorting inside her assuredly didn't make her feel weak. No, tingly and excited and eager to see more of him. To trail her fingers over those same fascinating contours.

Mayhap hunger had her a trifle addled.

Except she'd felt these curious, disturbing, and wholly delicious sensations before.

Blaike had ignored the stirrings he'd roused when they met that night she was introduced to London society, and she'd danced with him: a quivery, jelly-kneed twit. She'd overlooked the peculiar flutters the many times he'd come across her path at assemblies and gatherings. Disregarded the flushes and pattering pulse at Bristledale Court where he was a house guest of her brother-in-law, and her dashed pulse had ran amuck whenever she saw him. Resolutely smothered every nuance of attraction on the voyage to France those many months ago, knowing full well nothing could come of her school-girl infatuation.

But now . . .?

Those suppressed feelings burst forth, much like a shaken bottle of Champagne, once uncorked. And there wasn't a blasted way in all of Christendom to harness them, much less force them back into quiet submission.

Glancing at the umber liquid in the bottle atop his desk, she cleared her throat. Maybe a tot of brandy was a good idea after all.

No, she needed steady hands and a mind not befuddled by spirits.

A distraction.

That was what they both needed.

Something mundane and harmless.

"Did you draw all of these sketches?" Arcing her hand, Blaike indicated the detailed illustrations displayed about the great cabin. "If so, you're incredibly talented."

She chattered on, not giving him a chance to answer, while studiously avoiding looking into his eyes. For when she did, she forgot what she was about, forgot all else except how much she wanted to kiss him.

"I have no skill for either drawing or painting. In fact, I'm abysmal at both." Which Madame Beaulieu pointed out with annoying regularity. "Have you ever considered turning your interests to shipbuilding?"

"Yes, I drew them. But no, I've never given it serious consideration. My grandfather taught me the skill before he died. He was a shipbuilder in Italy, but when his wife died, he moved my mother to England. I've always assumed he'd been presented an opportunity too good to refuse." Oliver made a waving motion. "I've many more rolled up and stored in that chest at the foot of my bed."

"How fascinating." She brushed the back of her hand over her forehead, and stared across the cabin, racking her memory. "I cannot remember her name, dash it all. But I do recall a discussion over supper one evening about an acquaintance of Heath's—a shipping heiress."

Blaike squinted her eyes, searching her memory. "Lady somebody. She lives in Scotland, I believe. If you ever decide to pursue designing vessels or need additional suppliers, she might be a good person to contact."

Listen to her, nattering on like a lonely tabby.

Or a nervous woman much too attracted to a man

she shouldn't be.

"You didn't answer my question about why you and your sister are not at school." Oliver grasped a curl she'd missed pinning back into place and gave it a slight yank.

"And I'm not going to. Now, lie back so I can tend to your injury."

How hard could it be to clean and bandage the wound?

Instead of laying down, Oliver grasped her chin between his thumb and forefinger, and tenderly turned her face upward.

"Are you in some sort of trouble, Blaike?"

The more respectable or powerful
a person is, the more certain you may be
that they have secrets they don't wish exposed.
~*Scruples and Scandals*
The Genteel Lady's Guide to Practical Living

"**Y**ou are. I can see it in your eyes and in the way you hold yourself, *cara*."

Oliver endeavored to disregard the cannon thunder in his head and the fire poker tormenting his shoulder. Good thing he was left-handed, else his recovery would be even more of a nuisance.

Winged brows drawn taut, Blaike searched his face, hers a bevy of clashing emotions.

Mindful he'd breached decorum by touching her so intimately, he lowered his hand to his lap. He had few close friends, and he didn't need Ravensdale or Leventhorpe calling him out for overstepping the bounds.

Though for her, it might be worth the blasted risk.

The contour of Blaike's satiny skin pulsed in

Oliver's palm, and he balled his fist as much to preserve the sensation as to prevent himself from caressing the petal softness again. Or embracing her with his uninjured arm and soothing the tension from her shoulders and worry from her usually smooth forehead.

A faint fragrance, floral soap and the merest hint of vanilla, surrounded her.

Fresh and light, yet subtly tempting. It both aroused and soothed at once.

Much like her.

Skepticism or perhaps leeriness hovered around the fringes of her striking eyes as they roved his face. Those eyes that previously had been so vibrant and teeming with keen intelligence.

Abraham might've caused some of the distrust, but Oliver recognized a damaged soul.

Didn't he face one in the looking glass every day?

He coiled his hand tighter to keep from brushing her arm in a comforting gesture. If he had the right, he'd do so for the rest of his life, but their stations were too far apart to even consider something so beyond the pale.

So utterly wonderful.

"Is there anything I can do to help?"

"No."

Curt. Final.

She didn't attempt to offer an explanation.

Whatever had occurred had caused her to retreat into herself, and anger at whoever or whatever had made her suspicious, kicked angrily behind his ribs.

Oliver wasn't quite ready to quit the field just yet

She'd been so excited about continuing her education, and something had happened to change that as well as to steal her *joie de vivre*. The joy of life that used to put the rosy hue on her high cheeks, the radiant glow on her face, and the blue-violet glimmer in her eyes had faded into distrust. And he'd be bound, a degree of chagrin lingered there, too.

"May I presume the academy proved a disappointment?"

He leaned against the pillows and crossed his ankles, silently cursing the pain and weakness that forced him to do so.

Blaike's expression grew shuttered, snuffing out the vulnerability she'd exposed, and she dropped her focus to the whisky bottle in one hand and the cloth in her other.

"Let's just say *Les Dames de l'Académie de Grâce* wasn't at all what Blaire and I had anticipated. We're well rid of the place and a few of the people there, too."

He made an affirming sound in his throat.

Much more to that story he'd vow, but it was hers to tell in her own time.

Finished sanitizing her hands with the whisky, she'd wiped each instrument down with the spirit too, then laid them on a clean cloth atop the small storage chest turned bedside table.

"I heard you say you've never dressed a wound. You don't' have to do this." Oliver flicked his fingers toward his shoulder. "I can easily have one of the men tend me."

Hurt and confusion flitted across her features before she shrugged. "If you'd prefer—"

"No, I do not prefer, *cara*."

He almost caught her hand in his before he stopped himself. Not only wasn't it wise, to do so would betray the secret he'd guarded these many months. Besides her hands were sterile; at least as much as they could be in this environment. "I just don't want you to feel pressed into doing something you don't want to."

Her eyes narrowed for the briefest moment, and something akin to anger glinted there.

"I've vowed never to let that happen again, so you are safe in that regard, Oliver. But you are correct. I've never doctored a wound before. I shall understand if you want someone with more knowledge to treat you. Except, I've been given to believe your new cook has no experience treating anyone aboard ship either. Perhaps Mr. Hawkins? He seems most capable."

Though her speech was strong, and she met his gaze head-on, he detected more susceptibility beneath her admission. Perhaps he even detected a reluctance to leave him to another's care?

Oliver's manly pride swelled at the notion, no matter how misplaced.

Not that he blamed her in her hesitancy to leave him in Fairnly's incapable hands. The cook was an unfriendly, unbathed cawker, and within a week he'd alienated almost every crew member with his superior attitude. Given a choice, he'd be Oliver's last pick for a nursemaid. Fairnly was superstitious, as well, and Oliver would be bound, he hadn't been pleased to learn two women now traveled with them.

"Fairnly was hired for his cooking skills and naught else."

And only until Oliver could replace him. It had either been Fairnly or no cook until they reached London. As capable and loyal as Oliver's crew were, even they wouldn't have taken kindly to a diet of hardtack for a month or more.

"If you're certain . . .?"

Was that a pleased smile playing around the edges of her pink mouth?

"I'd far prefer your presence to his. You smell much nicer. He reeks of sour ale, garlic and onions, and it's not only because he's the cook. I think there's something foul in the bag he wears around his neck." After winking, Oliver closed his eyes and folded his hands across his abdomen. "I shan't move or even flinch until you're done."

Cloth in hand, she dabbed at his shoulder, and he nearly choked on his swiftly indrawn breath. From the hell-fired burning, he'd vow whisky dampened the piece she applied to his flesh.

"Well, you'll have to move. Else I shan't be able to wrap the bandage around your back, unless someone helps me," she teased lightly.

He'd gargle freshly-cast bullets before uttering a sound of distress, even if the very devil himself stabbed Oliver's shoulder unmercifully this moment.

"Oliver?"

"*Hmm?*" He couldn't manage much more without gasping or cursing.

"Thank you for coming to our aid. You wouldn't be hurt if you'd not been so chivalrous. I realized on the way to the *Sea Gypsy* that you weren't asked to provide passage for us to London, else I presume Lieutenant Drake would've been with you. I had assumed—" She gently daubed at his shoulder. "Well, never mind."

He cracked an eye open, his imbecilic heart leaping within his chest at the breathtaking smile she bestowed on him.

To be able to claim a woman such as her for a life-time.

Now there was fanciful thinking.

Sisters-in-law to marquises and wards of earls did not marry uneducated bastards with empty coffers. Men who called the sea their home and hadn't elsewhere but their ships to lay their heads except for the generosity of his friends on occasion.

Not exactly truth, that. Willoughby had often issued an invitation, as had Oliver's half-brother and sisters. Of course he'd refused, but he also knew deep inside, his rejection of his father would've saddened *Mamma*.

He shut his eyes again, lest he betray himself further. Truth to tell, he was exhausted, and wanted nothing more than to sleep for four and twenty hours.

Ballocks to that.

He wanted Blaike more, but that wasn't ever going to happen.

Catching up on his sleep would have to wait until the *Sea Gypsy* made the Mediterranean Sea. Not much respite to be had, however, before she sailed into the Bay of Biscay, and then they'd best pray for favorable weather. Many a ship had foundered during a tempest in those unpredictable waters.

"Have you any news from home?" Blaike glanced

upward, melancholy shadowing her face. "I've missed everyone horribly. Brooke's baby boy arrived the second week of February. I cannot wait to see little Leopold. Have you seen him? Blythe is due in May, and Brette a few months later, I believe."

Fertile bunch those Culpeppers.

What joy it would be to see Blaike's belly round as Oliver's child grew within her. Such fantasies were for fools.

"I haven't had the pleasure of meeting the future Earl of Ravensdale yet. Drake's resigned his commission. Familial obligations." He could've bitten off his tongue for revealing that.

Why couldn't he have blathered something trivial: Gunter's had a new ice flavor or that the king had packed on another stone?

She paused in her preparations, giving him a wide-eyed look. "Oh, I hope nothing unfortunate has occurred."

"His family is landed gentry, and his older brother was shot dead—a hunting accident." Or so everyone was being told. Drake wasn't convinced. "He left behind an . . . ah . . ."

Damned awkward. Should've kept his mouth shut.

Oliver ought not to have mentioned Drake's situation, devil it. Especially since Drake had cast his eye on Blaire months ago, and she'd obviously returned his regard.

Blaike held up a wicked-looking needle, and Oliver broke out into a cold sweat.

She set the miniature spear aside. "We won't be needing that, I don't think."

Thank God.

In the last few hours, he'd called upon God more than he had in his entire life.

"Did he leave behind a wife? Children?" Sympathy creased the edges of her eyes. "So tragic when death strikes someone so young."

"No, a betrothed in a . . . delicate condition." No need for her to tell him his cheeks glowed.

Why did discussing pregnancy turn even the most stalwart of men into stammering milksops?

"Oh, dear. That's most unfortunate. Whatever will she do?" Blaike hadn't judged harshly, as most would a woman in that situation, but instead had shown compassion.

Should he tell her?

She might as well know, so she could tell Blaire, since it was possible Drake would've made a decision by the time they reached London. The next time any of them saw him, he might well be married.

"The last I heard, Drake—*ever the noble chap*—

was considering, albeit reluctantly, taking his brother's place. That way the child, if a son, could claim his rightful inheritance."

Blaike's face fell, and she dropped her gaze to the floor, but not before he saw the devastation for her twin in her eyes. "That is very benevolent of him."

"He's a true gentleman, to be sure."

Drake was considering marrying to protect the reputation and lineage of a child that wasn't his, while Oliver's own titled father had never once offered *Mamma* marriage. Bitterness Oliver had striven to dispel for years coiled 'round his belly.

Not for himself; he didn't want anything from Willoughby.

But his mother had loved him until she drew her last breath. Even as a small child he knew she adored Willoughby. Dangerous to love like that. It warped common sense and reason.

Shut up, he ordered his morose thoughts.

Ruminating on the past only tainted the future. Instead, he concentrated on the alluring woman in his quarters. Much more pleasurable and certainly not likely to be repeated on another voyage.

Blaike resumed puttering about, talking to herself every now and again.

He ticked his mouth upward.

What a delight she was.

M'Lady Lottie must've finally gone to sleep. He cringed to think how Blaike would react if she heard the bird's most flamboyant phrases. It might be a good idea to teach Lottie some new, less unsavory quotes, as Hawkins had advised.

"Here, Oliver."

Dragging his eyelids upward, he found Blaike hovering over him, her small bosoms, stained with his blood, dangerously close to his face.

What had he done to deserve this torment?

Hawkins would, no doubt, have an opinion as to that.

With determination that would've made a monk proud, Oliver averted his avid attention. He forced his gaze to stay above her chin.

Blaike held a tumbler filled with a generous portion of brandy. "I've decided you should have something for the pain while I tend you. I'm sure it will still hurt, but perhaps a little less."

Anything to numb his raging senses.

He gulped the strong spirit down, and the next glass too. He welcomed the burning in his belly, and even more the languid warmth spreading through his veins.

No. What he welcomed more than anything was Blaike's sweet touch upon his naked flesh.

"I'm in your capable hands, *cara mio.*"

"*Cara mio*?" She gave him a perplexed look. "Is that Italian? What does it mean?"

"It is. My mother and grandfather spoke Italian at home, and naturally, I learned to as well." Oliver didn't answer the second question since he had no right to call her by any endearment. He raised her hand to his mouth and kissed the knuckles, sanitation be hanged. "I trust you."

A proper lady is at no time honor-bound to keep a
depraved secret nor compelled to reveal a joyous one.

~Scruples and Scandals
The Genteel Lady's Guide to Practical Living

8

Hours later, Blaike pressed the back of her hand
against Oliver's cool forehead.

He didn't feel hot, but what if he developed a fever?

She hadn't considered that possibility. Keeping the
wound sterile had been her chief concern. Other than to
wash him down with cool water, she had no idea how to
treat a fever.

Heat skated up her cheeks at the notion of bathing
his nakedness, and she pressed her hands to her face as
she spun away from him.

Her gaze fell on the volume Mr. Grover had
brought up with the medical chest.

Surely the book mentioned how to treat fevers.

Her panic subsided, and as she studied one of
Oliver's drawings, she finished eating the dried plum
she'd been nibbling.

Mr. Hawkins had brought up a tray hours earlier.

Simple fair: Bread, cheese, cold meat, fruit, and tea.

She'd enjoyed every bite, until she remembered Oliver's growling stomach before she dosed him with brandy. The laudanum hadn't been necessary, but now she fretted that maybe she shouldn't have allowed him to sleep until they knew for certain he hadn't been concussed.

Thrashing about in his agitation, he mumbled in his sleep again.

Something about Abraham.

A history existed between those two, she'd vow. Something ugly from the extreme animosity they held for each other.

Yawning, she glanced around Oliver's quarters again.

Only one lamp remained lit on the desk.

When she'd returned from changing her gown and looking in on Blaire, fast asleep in her berth, she found Mr. Hawkins had put the lights out. He'd also tucked Oliver beneath the bedclothes after removing his boots, straightened the cabin, and removed the bloody cloths and clothing.

A true gem, was Mr. Hawkins.

She'd wager not every first mate tended to his captain as if he were his son.

M'Lady Lottie occasionally made little chirping noises, but hadn't screamed anymore blush-worthy expressions.

Arching her back, Blaike stretched her arms overhead. Lord, she was exhausted.

The ship's gentle, rhythmic rocking revealed they'd left *Port de Lyon*.

She'd scarcely paid attention to the shouting and other noises above deck as the crew prepared to weigh anchor. Her entire focus had centered on treating Oliver's wound. It wasn't as deep as she'd first feared, and surely a man as young and strong *and virile*, as he would make a quick recovery.

When another large strand of hair slipped loose from its pins, she blew out a frustrated sigh. Might as well unpin the whole mass then.

Using the looking glass attached to Oliver's washstand, Blaike removed the pins. She tried running her fingers through the length, but encountered several snarls. Upon spying his hairbrush, she boldly snatched it up, then returned to her chair positioned beside his bed.

His black, slightly wavy locks sharply contrasted with the white pillow. The ribbon tying his hair had gone missing on the way to the ship. She rather liked his shoulder length mane. It fit the dashing, pirate image she'd first formed about him.

A romantic at heart, she'd secretly harbored girlish fancies since meeting him at her very first *le beau monde* gathering.

Oliver would fall passionately in love with her and whisk her away on his ship, she fantasized. They'd sail around the world, visiting exotic places, happy as grigs. And when the children came along—three, no make that four—he'd gladly forfeit his carefree life. They'd settle on a cozy farm in the country; perhaps raise sheep or dairy cattle.

Yes, he'd be the buccaneer turned gentleman farmer.

That was before she'd seen his drawings though. He'd never be content planting corn or herding sheep.

She skewed her mouth into a slight pout.

That wasn't the life she craved either—except for that part about sailing from port to port. She'd perish from tedium on a farm, but neither did living an idle life in London, flitting from once social assembly to another, appeal.

Why Blaike was so discontent, she didn't know.

If the world were a fair place, and women weren't considered inferior to men, she'd attend university. Become a scholar or a barrister or a politician. Maybe even a physician or a ship's navigator. Now those careers sounded exciting, and she'd be able to use her intellect, mayhap learn several other languages, too.

Although, vernaculars didn't seem her strong-suit.

Of course, children would be lovely, but she wanted more from life than darning socks, baking pastries, endless needlework, and wiping adorable turned-up noses.

This dissatisfaction had grown since she left Esherton Green. At times such frustration overwhelmed her, she wanted to rail at the injustice. To do so would be futile; she and Blaire had already been given more opportunity than most women.

As Blaike watched the even rise and fall of Oliver's chest, she ran the brush through her hair. She'd always found the action soothing, and soon, drowsiness engulfed her. Oh, to be in her comfortable, sparse bedroom at Esherton, tucked beneath her worn quilt. Life at Esherton hadn't been easy, but it had been safe.

Sedate. Predictable.

And boring as aged, snoozing cats.

She closed her eyes, and allowed her head to droop to her chest. Sleep beckoned, but she feared leaving Oliver, and other than Hawkins, commanding the ship at present, she didn't trust anyone else to watch him.

"Blaike."

She jerked her head up. "Yes, Oliver?"

He slept on, but she touched his brow again just to be sure it wasn't hot.

What agitated him so that even after drinking nearly three full tumblers of brandy on an empty stomach, he muttered in his sleep?

If he hadn't intervened on her and Blaire's behalf, he wouldn't be injured.

A shudder rippled down her spine, and she swallowed.

Thank heavens he'd come along, or at this moment, instead of anticipating a joyful homecoming, she and her twin would be sailing to a horrific fate. Blaike would've thrown herself into the ocean before enduring a lifetime as a sex slave.

Utter nonsense his vowing he deserved to be shot. Meunier was the one who'd earned a hole in his shoulder. Oliver judged himself too harshly.

Yawning again, she wistfully eyed the big bed while setting the hairbrush on the night table anchored to the floor.

Did she dare?

Why not?

There was plenty of room. No one would know, save she.

Fully dressed, except for her half-boots, of course, she'd rest beside Oliver, and if he stirred, she'd be right there. No one could suggest anything untoward had occurred. How could it possibly anyway, when he was injured? For certain his crew would be grateful that their captain was so well cared for.

True, she shouldn't be in his quarters unchaperoned, but neither should she and Blaire have traveled from Geneva without a companion.

Once Blaike had settled herself comfortably— beneath the coverlet, yet atop the other bedding—she closed her eyes. Taking care not to bump Oliver or wake him as he softly snored, she relaxed into the pillows with a long sigh.

Her mind turned to the worry that had plagued her for days now.

"How am I going to explain why we left Geneva?"

"Why did you?"

Oliver's whispered question almost had Blaike tumbling off the bed. She turned her head to study him, his dear face mere inches from hers.

He was awake now and not talking in his sleep.

"Oh, Oliver, I didn't mean to waken you." She touched his chest, almost yanking her hand away as little sparks of sensation where she'd encountered crisp hair skittered all the way up her arm. "Do you hurt? There's laudanum—"

"No. The pain is bearable." After staring at her hand for a long moment, he entwined his fingers with hers, then cast the cage a fleeting glance. Her skin was so pale beside his tanned flesh. "If we keep our voices down, M'Lady mightn't awake yet."

"And squawk something else embarrassing?" Blaike whispered.

"Exactly. What time is it?" He shifted to look out a window. "We're underway?"

She lifted a shoulder. "I'm not certain of the time. Early morning I should think, and yes, we've been underway for a while. I'm sorry I woke you." She apologized again.

"You didn't. I habitually awake and rise early." Oliver glanced around his cabin before his scrutiny came to rest upon her. He gave her fingers a little squeeze. The gesture comforting and natural.

"What has you so tormented, Blaike?"

Perhaps it was exhaustion; or shock from the terrifying encounter with Captain Abraham; or relief that Oliver hadn't slipped into unconsciousness; or simply the need to tell someone what she'd stuffed into a dark, remote niche and feared to utter, but tears leaked from her eyes.

The hot drop trailed over her cheeks, slowly at first, then ever more swiftly.

She turned her face away and tried to extract her hand.

Rather than releasing her, Oliver pulled her nearer, urging her to lay her head in the crook of his uninjured arm.

"Come, *dolcezza*. I still have one good shoulder you can cry on."

His voice had the merest slur. The effects of the liquor or sleepiness? Pray not his head injury.

The temptation proved too great.

With a ragged sob, she yielded. One arm wrapping around his waist, she folded into his side and pressed her face into his strong, wonderful smelling flesh.

"*Cara mia*," he murmured into her hair. "Sometimes the telling of secrets sets one free."

She shook her head. "Not in my case. I'm afraid I'm ruined, Oliver."

He stiffened for an instant.

Shocked by her admission?

Then how could she tell him the whole sordid account?

He pressed his mouth to the top of her head and ran his strong fingers through her hair. The caress soothed as well as stimulated. A dangerous combination.

"I cannot fathom such a thing. Tell me what has happened, and we'll contrive a solution."

Blaike couldn't bear to look at him. To see the disgust or accusation in his eyes. With her face still tucked into the corner of his shoulder, she whispered, "I was foolish and gullible."

The words came forth, one painful utterance at a time. While he simply nodded or made comforting sounds, the awful story spilled from her lips.

"I suspected something sinister was afoot, almost since we arrived at *Les Dames de l'Académie de Grâce*. But everyone was so closed-mouthed. Afraid to speak their suspicions. Far too many gentleman were invited to dine with us, to join us for musicals, to play cards or charades, or to attend dances at the academy for my peace of mind. Often male guests would disappear halfway through the evening, sometimes reappearing, but usually not."

"You think the school is a front for something else?"

Even his breath warming her scalp brought succor to her harrowed soul.

"I'm convinced it is. There were women there, in another house, who never attended lessons. Supposedly, they were former students who'd accepted offers of employment from Madame Beaulieu. Seamstresses, milliners, lace-makers, that sort of thing. We were told they did so because their schooling had ended, and they didn't want to go home. Or else their tuitions hadn't been paid, and Madame demanded compensation."

Blaike rubbed at her wet cheeks, then took the edge of the sheet and dried her face before dabbing Oliver's damp shoulder.

"I'm sorry. I've soaked you." She turned onto her side, and after sweeping her hair out of the way, pulled a pillow beneath her head.

He grasped a handful of her hair and brought it to his face. He closed his eyes and brushed his cheek. "I adore your hair. I've never seen any lovelier. Moonbeams and stars and silver and fairy sparkles and all sorts of wondrous things must've been used to create the color."

"Fairy sparkles, *hmm*? I rather like that, I think."

Quite the romantic, wasn't he? Another lovely thing about her swashbuckler.

His hair, on the other hand, was midnight black. So dark that it appeared almost blue in some light. Tilting her head upward, she asked, "Are you sure I'm not causing your other shoulder pain?"

Oliver's mouth tipped into a tender smile. Dark stubble shadowed his neck and cheeks above and below his tidy beard.

She found the bristles quite enticing.

"I'm fine, and a few tears aren't likely to harm me. I'm made neither of salt nor sugar, so it's unlikely I'll melt." He chuckled, that wondrous deep rumble, and moved his hand to her back, brushing his fingertips up and down her spine. "About your concerns at the academy. Not exactly forthright of the headmistress, but I don't know that she did anything illegal, *cara*."

"That's what I thought at first, as well. Until a pattern emerged. A girl would attend supper when we had male guests. However, the next day, we'd be told she'd departed or chosen to enter Madame Beaulieu's service." Blaike idly plucked at his coverlet, replaying those final days at the academy in her head.

"Then, a certain gentleman, Jonathon Severs, started paying marked attention to me. The headmistress kept pairing us at dinner, for the entertainment, and so on." Mouth turned down, she scrunched her nose in remembered disgust. "He was much too forward, making vulgar insinuations, touching me, and trying to get me alone. Blaire and I cried off attending functions, but if we didn't put in an appearance, we weren't fed. If it hadn't been for my sister's constant presence, I know not what might have happened."

"I thought you'd both lost weight. So this Madame

Beaulieu basically used extortion to force you to cooperate with her matchmaking?" Though Oliver continued to gently caress her shoulders and back, rage tinged his mild inquiry.

"Yes. When we still resisted, she fabricated some codswollop about our tuition being tardy. I knew that to be a bald-faced lie. Heath paid the entire two years' room, board, and tuition in advance. He made sure Blaire and I knew that when he gave us pocket money for fripperies or fallalls. It's that money we'd hid away and used to hire the coach and pay for the inns when we fled the academy."

"But why did you have to flee? Couldn't you have written a letter home?"

"We—I—did. And Blythe responded that she'd made passage arrangements. That's why I first thought that you . . ." She cast him a swift glance, only discerning concern and interest in his ebony gaze.

"Anyway, the night we fled, I was foolhardy. I followed one of the new girls and a gentleman who'd often been Madame Beaulieu's guest out into the garden courtyard. I should've waited for Blaire to return from the necessary, but I was afraid for Maria. She was only fifteen. The evening was too cold for a walk in the gardens, but a pathway led to the other house, and I feared that's where he meant to take her. I should've known it was a trap when Jacqueline Severs made a point of telling me Maria had been escorted outside."

Oliver stilled his caresses for a moment. "Another Severs? Related to Jonathon, I presume?"

Blaike nodded, drawing in a shaky breath.

"His sister, and every bit as evil as her brother. There's something distinctly off, truly queer, about those two." Even now, recalling what transpired next turned her skin to ice, made her flesh crawl, and she felt on the verge of casting up her simple dinner.

She shivered, and Oliver nudged her closer to his strong warmth.

"What happened?"

"I'd no sooner left the veranda, than Jonathon was upon me. Groping and pawing, tearing my gown."

Eyes pinched closed, she relived the terror.

"With one hand clamped over my mouth, he tried to drag me behind a row of shrubberies, but we Culpeppers are no small misses, except for Brette, that is. I fought him, but he managed to throw me to the ground. He—"

At the memory, she trembled head to toe.

"He climbed on top of me, and . . ."

A decorous lady holds fast and buries
any secrets that can harm innocents, but readily
share secrets which bring joy and happiness.

~Scruples and Scandals
The Genteel Lady's Guide to Practical Living

9

Blaike shuddered, once again experiencing the revulsion and terror.

Oliver hugged her tightly to his chest and whispered fiercely, "I'll kill the cur if I ever come across him. I swear, I shall."

"I thought he was going to ravish me. I wanted to die."

"He . . . didn't?"

Did relief weight his question?

"Almost, but just before—"

She had to stop for a moment and take a calming breath.

Every time she thought of that night, she re-experienced the awfulness.

"His sister, Blaire, and Madame Beaulieu

interrupted. "I don't know whether it was by chance or by design, but to everyone, it looked as though I'd been compromised. I fear if Blaire hadn't been there also, those other two might have let him finish."

Would've cheered him on, the depraved pair.

"I still feel so soiled."

"Blaike," Oliver nudged her chin upward until she met his tender gaze in the dimness. The lone lamp's weak glow added an almost romantic aura to the great cabin. "You were the victim of what I'm quite confident is an ongoing scheme to despoil women and force them into prostitution. You were only trying to help Maria."

"I was, and it makes me ill that I don't know what became of her. If indeed she was even outside that evening." She stared at the overhead beams. "We should've left the academy and alerted the authorities as soon as we suspected something afoul was taking place. But everyone at home was so proud of us. And such a vile accusation needed absolute proof. We didn't trust Madame Beaulieu not to concoct some plausible excuse either."

He folded her into his embrace once more.

Nothing before had ever felt as effortless or right.

Oliver might not be of noble birth or be able to list prestigious universities he attended, but he was an honorable, decent man. She'd take that over the other characteristics in a heartbeat.

He spoke into her hair. "You'll have to tell your family, *bella*. Madame Beaulieu mustn't be allowed to continue."

"I know." And she would, as soon as they reached London. Oliver was right. Madame Beaulieu must be stopped. A wonder her duplicity had gone undetected this long. How many innocent girls had met their ruin at the academy?

M'Lady Lottie ruffled her feathers, making a throaty, purring sound, and Blaike held her breath lest the bird start her shattering screaming. After a moment, when the cockatoo remained quiet, she relaxed.

Oliver shifted slightly, his firm thigh bumping hers and causing a fascinating jolt to streak up her leg.

"I'm curious." He smothered a yawn. "How is it this Miss Severs escaped the same destiny as the others?"

Blaike pondered his question for several long moments.

Yes, just how had Jacqueline escaped that fate?

"I suspect she and her brother must've been co-collaborators with Madame Beaulieu." A yawn forced its way past her lips as well, and overcome with drowsiness, she burrowed deeper into his sculpted side.

"Might I ask you a question, too, Oliver?"

He moved his head a touch, making a drowsy, affirmative noise.

Did she dare?

It wasn't her business, and she didn't want him to think she was poking her nose into something that concerned only him. That was exactly what she was doing, though.

"I suspect there's deep animosity between you and Captain Abraham that goes beyond what he wanted to do with Blythe and I."

He went rigid.

"*Cara mia*, that's a statement, not a question."

Eyes remaining shut, Oliver ran his fingertips the length of her arm from shoulder to elbow, then back again. He cracked an eyelid, and gave her an undecipherable look, then sighed, his reluctance tangible.

The ship's gentle swaying had lulled Blaike half-asleep.

"Never mind. I shouldn't have asked." She settled a jot deeper into her pillow. How easy it would be to slumber here. "You need to rest in any event."

"I don't mind telling you. The tale's ugly, however."

Oliver paused for such an extended moment, she believed he'd changed his mind.

Finally, he exhaled a long, troubled breath.

"When I was thirteen, I came home one evening from delivering a letter to a ship's captain for my *nonno*—my grandfather. I discovered him dead beside his desk, a wicked ivory-handled dagger protruding from his chest."

Blaike couldn't prevent her distressed half-cry, half gasp.

Why had she asked? Snooped into Oliver's personal affairs?

He needed to recover, not have old emotions and trauma stirred once more. Particularly those caused by the spawn of Satan now locked in Lyon's jail.

"A man—Abraham—was tearing the place apart." Oliver stared overhead, as if seeing the horrific scene again. "The contents of the shelves and desk drawers were strewn all over the floor, and he'd even yanked drawings and signs from the walls. I thought him a burglar. Determined to kill him for murdering *Nonno,* I jumped on his back. Using the scrimshaw knife my grandfather had gifted me at Christmastide, I slashed his face.

So that was how the cur acquired his scar.

"I'm so sorry, Oliver. It must've been horrible and tragic for you, and I overstepped when I asked." She pressed her flattened hand to his chest, his strong heartbeat pulsing against her palm. "Please, you needn't tell me anymore. I see how painful it is for you."

He tightened his fingers on her arm for a second. "I haven't talked to anyone about that night."

Her heart gave a queer skip.

Was he doing so now because he felt as safe and comfortable with her as she did with him?

"I was a skinny, undersized waif, and he shook me off like a week-old kitten attacking a boarhound. When I landed, I hit my head on the corner of the desk," Oliver pointed at his L-shaped hairline scar, "and was knocked senseless."

"Dear God," she breathed, stricken by Abraham's evilness.

"You'll think I'm dicked in the nob, Blaike, but I swear I was roused by my mother calling my name, over and over."

"I don't think that's fanciful at all, Oliver. There's much in this world that cannot be explained."

A rough sound, part grunt, part confirmation, echoed in the back of his throat. "Flames were already climbing the front walls when I came to. I'm convinced Abraham knocked the lamp over deliberately. Fires always follow in his wake."

Jaw slack, she jerked her head up. "He meant to kill you too, the fiend!"

"Apparently." He sounded more resigned than weary or angry.

"But why, Oliver? What does he have against you? Or your grandfather?"

A few strands of his surprisingly silky hair tickled her nose, and she brushed them away. Then balled her hand against the temptation to press her lips to the pulse ticking in his corded neck.

A swell lifted the ship, and she rolled a smidgeon closer to him. She didn't bother scooting away.

"That, *cara*, is something I've asked myself for half my life now. And I'm no closer to an answer than I was that night. Unless he truly was a thief and after the contents of the desk's hidden drawer, though there wasn't a whole lot there. I managed to collect *Mamma*'s jewelry—just emerald and diamond embedded hair combs and a matching pendant, ring, and earrings. I was always fascinated with them as a child."

He gazed into the distance as if seeing another time and place. "She was so beautiful wearing them. Right before she died, she said I should gift the parure set to my wife."

"How did she die?" It was brazen of Blaike to ask. "I lost my parents in a carriage accident."

"Childbirth. Another son. He only lived a few hours. My sire—Viscount Willoughby—insisted on paying for the burial costs."

"Oh."

Bitterness deepened Oliver's voice when he mentioned his father, and Blaike wasn't about to poke that wound, too.

The subject was understandably difficult for him.

He cleared his throat. "Before escaping out the back door, I also grabbed a few of *Nonno's* drawings as well as the rest of the secret drawer's contents. There wasn't much. Only a leather-bound packet containing documents and letters written in Italian and a small bag of coins."

Tears blurred Blaike's vision. Oliver truly might've died.

No wonder he despised Captain Abraham.

"That money is what I used to survive until I convinced a captain to hire me on as a cabin boy, even though I was really too old for the position. On this very ship, as a matter of fact. I keep the jewelry, packet, and the drawings in a secret compartment in my chest's false bottom." He flicked a calloused finger toward the end of the bed where the trunk sat and, yawning, shifted his legs again.

"Do you know what the documents are?" If his grandfather kept them hidden with money and gems, might they be valuable or important?

"No. I don't read Italian, and moreover, a sailor doesn't have coin enough to spare to hire a reputable fellow to translate them. So I've never had them interpreted."

"Had I been you, my curiosity would've nearly killed me, not knowing what they said." She'd never been altogether patient with puzzles or riddles.

He twisted his mouth up on one side. "I figured if they were truly important, *Nonno* would've told me about them. I've only even glanced at them once or twice. They still smell of smoke and the memories of that night—"

She rushed to change the subject. "So it was just you and your grandfather then?"

Here they lay, chatting in hushed tones like intimate friends—*or lovers*—as if it hadn't been months since they'd last seen or spoken to each other. It seemed like yesterday they'd last spoke, so comfortable and contented was Blaike.

"Yes. My mother died when I was seven."

"I cannot conceive how hard that was for you." He must've been such a lonely child. "My sisters and I, our cousins too, lost our parents, but we had one another. I imagine you were very close to your grandfather then."

"Practically inseparable, except for the almost three years that I attended Eton. That was Willoughby's inflexible demand."

Ah, so that's why he disdained the man.

Oliver rubbed his nose, his mouth twisted into a cynical line. "I'm sure a few pockets were heavily lined for granting him the favor. I wasn't well received, being younger than the average chap in attendance and a by-blow to boot. Even children look down their well-bred noses at those born on the wrong side of the blanket."

Cruising over the waves, the ship echoed with creaks and the whoosh of the ship's bow meeting the ocean. Blaike found the subtle sounds relaxing, though an occasional bang from above or a resounding grate interrupted her reverie.

"It wasn't any fault of yours, Oliver. And look what you've accomplished." She waggled her fingers in the air to indicate the *Sea Gypsy*. "Quite remarkable, I'd say, for someone so young."

"I'll be eight and twenty in a few days, *cara*. I did meet Drake at Eton. We became fast friends at once."

A wicked chuckle shook his broad chest and quirked his mouth into that rapscallion grin she found so irresistible.

"I cannot count the number of instances he came to my defense," Oliver said. "Even planting a few good facers on my behalf. The last time, he broke Chatterley's squat nose, and Drake was sent down for good."

Rubbing between his eyebrows, he exhaled a deep breath. "So, I ran away. Home to *Nonno.*"

"And your father, the viscount? How did he take the news?"

Blaike's cousin, Brooke, had explained Oliver's circumstances when they'd first met him, and he'd proven himself an exemplary gentleman. She'd done so to remind the girls not to judge someone because of their birth or station in life.

Sternness sharpened his face. "He arrived at *Nonno's* office in his fancy coach, the Willoughby gold and blue coat of arms gleaming proud and bold against the glossy black paint. Every bit the nobleman accustomed to having his way, he ordered me back to school."

Oliver affected a lofty air and voice raised disdainfully, announced in a pretentious accent, "'The men in our family have always attended Eton until they go to university. I expect the same of you, young Oliver. Most especially since your instructors tell me you have an extraordinary talent for recall.'"

He shut his eyes once more, his derisive snort loud in the still cabin. "As if he had any right to tell me what to do."

Actually, the viscount could be admired for acknowledging his illegitimate son and sponsoring his education. But now wasn't the time to tell Oliver that, nor had she the right. Blaike had no idea how she'd feel if she'd been the illegitimate offspring of a noble. "But you didn't go?"

"I told him to bugger himself, for which *Nonno* made me apologize, and then he agreed to allow me to visit Willoughby thrice a year for a fortnight each time." Chin jutted, he squinted his eyes, appearing very much the intractable child. "*That* punishment far exceeded my offense."

"It seems to me your father wanted a relationship with you. Perhaps wanted to make amends for . . ."

Oliver speared her a sharp look.

Now she'd waded into it, bringing up that indelicacy. She cleared her throat. "What were they like? Your visits, I mean?"

"Willoughby was always thoughtful and kind, as were my half-brother and sisters. I cannot fault any of them in that regard." He scratched his nose as the call of a lone gull sounded. "Even now, I often receive invitations to one affair or another they are hosting. I never attend."

Someday she'd ask him why, but not today.

His last three words ended that thread of conversation as succinctly as if he'd said, "Mind your own business."

"What did he mean by your talent?" Pulling the coverlet over her shoulder, she also closed her eyes.

"I can see something once and remember it with great precision and detail." The revelation seemed more pained than proud.

It didn't take someone terribly astute to recognize the subject bothered Oliver. Though he'd answered her initial question, he'd raised numerous more. That discussion would have to take place later. He could scarcely keep his eyes open.

"Shut yer mouth." M'Lady Lottie muttered crankily. "Blasted dillberry maker."

"Oh dear. We've roused your cross bird." Blaike held her breath, hoping Lottie would go back to sleep. After a handful of minutes, when the cockatoo didn't say anything more, she relaxed.

Oliver had closed his eyes again, pain pinching the corners of his strong mouth.

Her hatred for Abraham rivaled that of hers for Jonathon Severs. Appalled and a mite frightened at the fury engulfing her, she pursed her lips. "I'd say you have good reason to despise Abraham. I hope he never gets out of jail." She raised up a few inches, and searched Oliver's wan face. Her curiosity demanded satisfaction.

"Why didn't he get punished for what he did?"

Oliver's eyes remained closed as he answered, fatigue etched in every word. "Years later when I learned his identity, I tried to have charges brought against him. Too much time had passed. And besides, the authorities said it was my word against his."

If he'd been a powerful lord, with coin to toss in their direction, they'd have acted, she'd be bound. "What do you think he was after?"

The edges of his eyes creased as he considered her question. "I honestly have no idea."

He fell silent, likely lost in disagreeable memories.

That'd teach her to pry in the future. Nevertheless, she'd learned much about this fascinating man, none of which shocked or dismayed her. If anything, what she'd discovered made her admire him more. He'd overcome much.

With a resigned little huff, she pressed two fingers just over the bridge of her nose.

"I really should go, Oliver. I've delayed far too long. This is most inappropriate."

He'd keep this breech of decorum to himself, she didn't doubt. Oliver wasn't the type to toss confidences of this nature about. And she'd be bound, he'd tuck away for safekeeping what she revealed about Madame Beaulieu and the Severs until she was ready to tell all.

Still, her limbs weighted with fatigue and

uncustomary serenity, she made no effort to rise.

"Oliver?" she mumbled against the marble wall of his chest.

Deep, even breathing revealed he'd fallen asleep once more.

Good. He'd find respite from those dreadful recollections.

Blaike ought to leave, but she hadn't been this content in a long while. Sighing, she snuggled closer, inhaling the scent that was uniquely him. She'd indulge a short while longer, for this opportunity surely wouldn't be repeated.

"*Ti amo*, Blaike," he mumbled. "I love you."

How many treasures
have been lost or lives ruined from a
careless slip of the tongue? A secret worth keeping
is a secret worth guarding, whether yours or another's.

~Scruples and Scandals
The Genteel Lady's Guide to Practical Living

10

"**G**rab yer ankles, wench."

Oliver bolted upright, and agony exploded in his shoulder and head.

"Holy God," he gasped, pressing his good hand to the pigeon egg-sized lump near his temple. He didn't know which was worse: his gut-wrenching hangover or the skull-cracking pain stabbing his noggin.

"Lord help me," he groaned, though it sounded more like a strangled croak than a prayer.

Would Hawkins chastise him for using the Lord's name in vain or praise him for a pathetic attempt at supplication?

M'Lady Lottie screeched loud enough to crack the beams again.

Only respect for McMaster kept Oliver from selling the annoying creature to the first street peddler who made an offer. That, and he knew Lottie would die from a broken heart. He couldn't be that cruel, despite her being a major inconvenience.

Her cage rattled violently. "Twattling peg-puff!"

"Lottie! Shut up."

He lowered his legs over the edge of the bed, his mind still sleep-befuddled.

"Shut yer trap. Shut yer trap." Furious flapping ensued, then angry banging. "I want out."

"Give me a minute." Having a bird her size careening about his quarters wasn't ideal, but when he took her topside, she loved to perch either on the poop deck's taffrail or the crow's nest. After climbing the rigging, she'd screech foul expletives and sexual innuendos, much to the crew's amusement.

Just then, his memory came crashing back, as forcefully as the cannon fire exploding in his head.

Blaike.

He tensed, then cautiously looked behind him.

No gorgeous, blue-eyed vixen lay there. He almost picked up the pillow and sniffed it to see if it smelled of vanilla to make sure she'd ever lain beside him.

Maybe he'd dreamed she'd been cradled in his arms when he fell asleep again.

He hadn't imagined her torrid tale of why she'd fled Geneva.

Anger, fierce and scorching sluiced through him. Severs better hope he never encountered Oliver. Or Ravensdale or Leventhorpe for that matter. All three possessed black tempers when it came to protecting their own.

Except Blaike wasn't Oliver's to protect.

Didn't matter.

In his heart she was and always would be.

He'd teach Severs a lesson he wouldn't soon forget.

"Ol-eeve? Ol-eeve?"

More irritated clanging resounded from within the cage. "Move yer arse."

"It's Ol-i-ver. And I am moving my arse, as you so crudely put it."

He quirked his mouth upward on one side. Now he was carrying on conversations with temperamental birds? M'Lady Lottie had started using his name, too. Well, her version of it. Perchance, that meant she was adjusting to McMaster's death.

Oliver squinted out the small wooden-framed panes.

The sun wasn't too terribly high, so he hadn't slept the day away. So much for seeing the *Sea Gypsy* on her way, however. Nonetheless, he'd spoken the truth when he'd said his crew was capable of sailing the ship without him. He couldn't ask for more reliable or skilled men, with one exception.

Fairnly.

Maybe Oliver would hire a cabin boy to look after M'Lady Lottie. He had to hire a surgeon anyway. A lad would like that assignment. He would've when he first took to sea. London had plenty of unfortunate lads who would leap at the chance to have a place to rest their head each night and a full belly, to boot.

Yes, that might be the answer to the bird he'd inherited and didn't have the heart to get rid of. He knew what it was like to have the only person who loved you die and leave you alone, homeless, and dependent on others.

With extreme caution, so as to not aggravate his pulsating shoulder or risk dislodging his head from his neck, he shuffled to M'Lady Lottie's cage. Once he'd pulled the quilt off, he unlatched the door, and she flew out.

After circling the stateroom thrice, she landed on her perch and proceeded to groom herself. One foot in the air, reminding him of some the less decorous things she'd witnessed in her former life, she trained her burgundy-brown eyes on him. "Go outside?"

"Yes, when I've dressed." He'd forego his shave

today. His hammering head couldn't even take Hawkins's gentle razor strokes.

Resting his hands on either side of the mahogany washstand, Oliver examined his shoulder in the looking glass. A neat bandage wrapped across his chest and around his back. Blaike had done remarkably well for her first attempt, and pride as well as appreciation blossomed behind his breastbone.

No hysteria, fainting, or weeping. Just cool composure, even though she hadn't known what she was doing. She was one strong woman, and by far, one of the most intelligent he'd ever met.

After splashing his face with water and brushing what tasted like burnt peat from his teeth, he tossed a towel over his unharmed shoulder and reached for his hairbrush. Only it wasn't in its usual place. Slowly scrutinizing his quarters, his gaze came to rest on his night table.

Breaking into a wide grin, he retrieved it.

Wasn't this interesting?

Amongst the boar bristles lay several silky, white strands. Blaike had used his brush. Such an intimate, domesticated thing to do. He couldn't erase his much-too-pleased grin.

"Outside!" M'Lady Lottie shrieked.

Would he ever become accustomed to her screams?

Oliver finished dressing, not without muttering several curses and getting his sore arm stuck for a minute. Now he understood why men had valets. With some care, he added a vest, a belt at his waist, but gave up trying to tie his hair back. Lastly, he drew on his boots, again uttering several colorful phrases that made M'Lady Lottie's language seem almost chaste.

Giving a short whistle, he held out his uninjured arm, and at once, she swept from her perch and landed on his forearm where he secured a strap to her ankle, lest she try to fly away. With clipped wings, she wouldn't get far, but he still fretted that she might end up in the ocean.

"Let's go, M'lady. I have a mind to see how my crew and passengers fare."

More on point, a particular captivating passenger.

He grabbed his hat from its hook beside the door and crammed it on his head as he made his way along the narrow passageway.

Once topside, he took a moment to survey his ship before seeing to feeding the cockatoo. In vivid blue and unexpectedly smooth waters, the *Sea Gypsy* flew along, the wind filling her sails, and leaving *Port de Lyon*, far behind them.

Excellent.

That placed them that much farther out of

Abraham's reach. He'd seek the revenge he vowed, and Oliver must get the Culpeppers to London without delay. The day was soon coming that either he or Abraham would not walk away from an encounter with one another.

On deck, Oliver inhaled the tangy sea air, bearing the merest hint of salt and fish, deep into his lungs.

His crew oiled the masts, repaired rigging or sails, or went about the dozens of other tasks required of a clipper. Men nodded, waving or calling hello as he passed. To a man, they appeared relieved to see him up and about.

"Good to see you, Cap'n." Hawkins trotted across the deck, three deep furrows ridging his forehead. "How are you feelin'?"

"Like I've been run over by a frigate and hungry as a hog. Although too much brandy last night has my stomach a mite wobbly."

He glanced at the sails, noted the bright sky strewn with a few feathery clouds, then satisfied all was at it should be, ran a hand down M'Lady Lottie's chest.

"Lottie luv," she chirruped before scampering up his arm and cuddling close to his good shoulder.

To his credit, Hawkins kept a straight face. "Your Miss Culpepper is yonder."

He pointed to the poop deck.

Blaike, enshrouded in a hooded emerald cloak, chatted gaily with Melville. He appeared to be showing her how to knot two pieces of rope. Whatever men had not become smitten on the first voyage would likely fall under her spell this crossing. Then, she'd have the entire lot wrapped around her dainty little finger.

"She's not my Miss Culpepper." Though Oliver did like the sound of it.

Still, it wouldn't do for the hands to get the wrong impression. As much as he wished it otherwise, there could never be anything between him and Blaike. For her sake. It wouldn't do for any sort of speculative tattle to start either. Seldom could inaccurate gossip or secrets ever be fully snuffed.

"As you say, Cap'n." His voice quivering with suppressed humor, Hawkins yanked his bright orange and red knitted cap lower over his elfin ears. "She hasn't broken her fast, either. Should I bring a tray up? I think she'd enjoy eatin' in the open. The weather's most pleasant, and you could share a picnic—"

"A picnic?" Just what was his first mate about? Oliver cocked a brow, and M'Lady took the opportunity to nip his ear. "Ouch, you she-devil. What was that for?"

"Her way of givin' you a kiss." Hawkins chuckled while pulling his earlobe. "She used to groom McMaster's hair and even peck his lips."

Oliver drew the line there. Not the least bit sanitary.

Besides, he didn't trust the cantankerous bird not to pierce his lip or gouge an eye. He gently moved her back to his forearm. McMaster had been much too lenient with the cockatoo, giving her time and attention Oliver, as captain, simply couldn't spare.

Maybe what she needed was a mate.

And have *two* of the noisy, demanding beasts on board?

Oliver would have to think long and hard on that.

His attention strayed to Blaike again.

She nodded and deftly twisted the ropes into what appeared to be a rolling hitch, though he couldn't be certain from this distance.

"Where's Miss Blaire?"

"The poor lass ails from seasickness." Hawkins waved his rough hand toward the fairly calm water. "I hate to think how she'll suffer if the weather turns petulant."

It likely would. If not in the Mediterranean, then almost certainly in The Bay of Biscay.

Hawkins shifted his feet and scratched his neck whilst sending Blaike a speculative glance. "About that picnic—"

"Fine." Oliver conceded, happy to seize any excuse to spend time with Blaike. "Have simple fare prepared.

Bread, porridge, boiled eggs, tea for Miss Culpepper and my usual spiced coffee should suffice."

He didn't think he could get anything else down, despite his empty stomach's gurgles and growls.

The fresh, albeit chilly wind, did much to clear his head, though did nothing for the constant thrum in his shoulder. Oliver made his way to the poop deck, mindful not to jostle his wound. "Good morning."

Blaike whipped around, and a becoming pink tinged her high cheekbones. "Good morning. How did you sleep?" A slight crease pulling her fair brows together, she dropped her gaze to his shoulder. "Did the bandages cause you any discomfort? You're not feverish or bleeding?"

"No fever or bleeding, and I slept well, which is why I'm so late rising."

No, he was late rising because he drank too much and a certain blonde siren had made herself comfortable in his bed, luring him back to slumber.

He couldn't recall the last time he'd yielded to the temptation to fall back to sleep. It just showed how much Blaike affected him. He'd best watch himself, or he'd find his well-laid plans tumbling bow over stern.

"Hawkins tells me you haven't broken your fast either, so he suggested we share a tray here. The weather may not hold, and when it turns, it won't be safe for you to come above." Why was Oliver rambling on, making excuses? Just ask her if she wanted to eat with him.

"I've only been up for a short while myself." The merest smudge of purplish-blue half circles shadowed her lower lashes. She pulled her cloak tighter, and smiled at M'Lady Lottie. "Poor Blaire finally drifted to sleep, and I didn't dare eat in our cabin for fear she'd smell the food and begin retching again. I hoped to have ginger tea prepared for her. If you have any on board, that is."

A breeze wafted by, teasing the curls over her forehead.

"I honestly haven't the slightest idea whether we do or not, but I can have Hawkins ask Fairnly."

Melville chuckled when he saw the cockatoo still trying to cuddle Oliver. "Looks like she's taken to you, sir."

"Might I pet her?" Blaike turned an inquisitive gaze to Oliver. "She's lovely, isn't she? Sort of peach tinted all over."

"Except for her language," he agreed. "Which, I believe you've already heard."

"Yes. She has a most *colorful* repertoire." Blaike chuckled, a pleasant melodious sound.

"She needs to get to know you before she'll accept your touch." Oliver withdrew a piece of apple from

M'Lady Lottie's cage. "Give her this."

M'Lady Lottie sidestepped down his arm, eager for the treat.

Blaike offered the fruit to the cockatoo, and M'Lady Lottie grasped it in her claws. "Tit over arse, she goes."

Rather than become offended, Blaike burst out laughing. "I had no idea a bird could learn so many words and phrases."

"You haven't heard her worst yet, I'm afraid." Oliver removed the strap from the cockatoo's foot, then set her on her perch, but left the door open.

"Won't she fly away?"

"No, her wings are clipped. But she'll climb every rope on this ship, given the chance. She's become stuck twice, too. I've had to rescue her, since she terrifies the rest of the crew."

M'Lady Lottie made a sound suspiciously like a person passing wind, followed by a loud burp. She bobbed her head as if proud of her achievements.

"Her talents are quite . . . erm . . . diverse, it seems." Blaike couldn't decide if she was more amused or appalled.

"Indeed." A boyish slant to his firm mouth, Oliver scratched his chin, then smoothed his beard. "Melville, can you find something to use as a makeshift table and seats for us?"

"Aye. Will crates do?"

Blaike nodded. "Yes, that would be perfect."

Another thing to admire about her.

Nothing pretentious or pompous about any of the Culpeppers, but Blaike seemed to genuinely not care about the niceties many of her station expected. Few ladies with her connections would be content to sit atop a turned over crate and dine with rough sailors milling about.

In short order, Melville had assembled their improvised dining area. M'Lady Lottie crawled up the outside of her cage after enjoying an assortment of treats, and Hawkins appeared with their tray.

He gave them a toothy smile and set their food on the box serving as their table. "Miss. Cap'n."

"Thank you." Oliver gave the lumpy porridge the once over with a dubious gaze. "Would you mind asking Fairnly if there's any ginger to make tea? It might help with Miss Blaire's *mal de mer*."

"Aye. Straightaway." Still grinning, and looking entirely too pleased with himself, he wandered away, whistling what Oliver knew to be a favored hymn.

After gracefully sinking onto a crate, Blaike draped a serviette on her lap.

"I was wondering if you'd teach me how to use

those interesting instruments I saw on your desk?"

Gifted is the lady who knows
what secrets to hold fast in her heart
and which mysteries are better off revealed.
~Scruples and Scandals
The Genteel Lady's Guide to Practical Living

11

Oliver went rigid.

Teach her?

M'Lady Lottie scampered down the side of her cage. "Cheeky wench," she said, erecting her coral-toned crest.

Showing off for Blaike, was she? Or jealous mayhap?

Blaike rotated to observe her.

"She almost seems to respond, doesn't she, Oliver?"

Did she realize she had addressed him by his given name again?

Yes, he was an intimate friend of her guardian and brother-in-law, but protocol should be observed. Nonetheless he found it incongruously pleasing that there was another area that she didn't regard as necessary. She was truly an original woman. Diamonds of the first water, her guardian had called the Culpeppers. But Blaike was more than an exquisite beauty. She possessed a brilliant mind, keen wit, and a charming sense of humor.

But then he already knew that about her.

Just one of the many reasons she intrigued and fascinated him. How was it possible to love someone so intensely, more with each passing day? Bewitched and besotted. That was what he'd become. And a hopeless, romantic fool.

Blaike, her head tilted at the adorable inquisitive angle that was hers alone, still waited for his response.

"Sometimes, I think she does understand and answers me. Or maybe she reacts to inflections in voices or certain words cue her responses. McMaster oft' boasted how intelligent she is, and he swore she conversed with him." Oliver swallowed a spoonful of gloppy, barely tepid porridge and shuddered.

Yes, seeking Fairnly's replacement took precedence when the *Sea Gypsy* docked in London.

Loathe to waste the food, he lifted another spoonful to his mouth. His stomach reacted rather violently to the globby mass.

Mayhap he should forgo breaking his fast until his

belly had decided it wasn't going to toss the unappetizing contents onto the decking. Instead, Oliver poured himself a cup of coffee.

"Would you like to try a taste of my coffee?" He angled the pot toward her cup. "It's *caffè d'u parrinu*. An Italian specialty made with Arabic coffee flavored with cinnamon and cloves. I confess, I drink far too much of the brew."

He'd personally taught Fairnly how to make the beverage. Poorly prepared food was one thing, but improperly prepared coffee bordered on sacrilegious.

"It sounds heavenly. I'd love to try a cup." She gave him a coquettish smile. "That must be why you smell like spices."

He didn't dare ask how she'd come by that knowledge.

After pouring a cup and passing it to her, he lifted his cup to his nose. Inhaling the soothing aroma, he took a savory swallow. Every time he smelled *caffè d'u parrinu*, the scent hurtled him back to his earliest memories of *Mamma and Nonno* sitting at the kitchen table, chatting in Italian, drinking the steaming beverage, and eating pizzelle, Oliver's favorite pastry.

"*Mmm*." Raising her cup to her nose, Blaike too sniffed. "It smells wonderful." After taking a sip she sighed in pleasure. "It's amazing. Such rich flavor, but not too strong. I'd like to try it with milk sometime."

"Alas, we've no cows below deck, else I'd rush to accommodate you." Oliver glanced about, and assured that no one would overhear him, leaned forward. "Did I dream it, or did I fall asleep with you beside me?"

Blaike fixed her attention on his face as fresh color rose on her ivory cheeks. Her gaze meshed with his for an extended, poignant moment.

Around them, the usual din of shipboard life continued, yet it seemed as if it was just the two of them, in this special time and place reserved for them alone. For this brief glimpse into each other's soul.

She fidgeted with her serviette before she too peered 'round.

No need to tell him she knew full well her reputation would suffer further if it became known she'd shared his bed, no matter how innocently.

Making a pretense of reaching for a boiled egg, she whispered, "I stayed until I was certain you were all right. But as you must know, I had to leave before I was discovered."

"Tuppence fer a tup," M'Lady Lottie announced in her sing-song voice.

Oliver's and Blaike's gazes locked again, but in amused shock this time.

"That's a first." He offered an apologetic upward

hitch of his lips. "I'm rather leery of what else she might say."

Blaike covered her mouth and giggled. "I know I shouldn't laugh, for she's truly awful, and I don't want to encourage her, but I suppose she's to be admired for her intelligence and aptitude."

"You used my hairbrush."

Oliver hadn't meant to blurt it out like that. Like an accusation.

"I . . ." A gust whipped by, almost pulling the hood from Blaike's head. She snatched at it, just managing to keep her hair covered, then shivered. Skewing her lips sideways, she gave him an adorable, contrite smile. "I did. Forgive me, please. I know it was intrusive of me."

"I don't mind." He took another sip of the strong coffee to help wash down the lingering taste of porridge. "Whatever I have is yours to use."

"That's most generous of you." The mischievous twinkle that so often used to sparkle in her gaze appeared. "So, will you teach me?"

Her face radiated excitement. Such eagerness glowed in her eyes and her cheeks made rosy from the stiff breeze.

He should say no to such flummery.

A man with a jot of common sense—and not a glutton for punishment—would have done.

Instructing Blaike in the intricacies of mapping and navigation meant spending intimate time with her, smelling her delicious essence, inadvertently touching her.

If Oliver possessed an iota of sense he'd deny her request.

He didn't have the time, he could argue.

It wouldn't be proper, he might contend.

But I want to.

And honestly, he was flattered that she'd showed an interest.

"I shall, but only when I have no other duties that need my attention."

She gave a delighted little clap and squeal. "Thank you!"

When she looked at him like that, there wasn't anything he wouldn't do for her.

God save him from himself.

Aye, and save him from sapphire-eyed goddesses smelling of vanilla.

Four afternoons later, Blaike and Blaire stood near the poop deck's rail, watching the crew prepare for a celebration.

Oliver's birthday was today, and in preparation for tonight's festivities, a few sailors had brought treasured musical instruments on deck. They included two fiddles, a tabor pipe, a pan flute, and a little guitar unlike anything Blaike had ever seen before.

A barrel of rum had been rolled out for the occasion, and Oliver had ordered extra rations for each sailor as well. She secretly hoped there might also be dancing, and that he'd request a waltz from her.

She'd wanted to do something special for him, since he'd basically saved the twins' lives, though he repeatedly denied doing so when she and her sister thanked him again. However, there was no practical way to bake any sort of a special treat.

Just as well, for Fairnly gave her the shivers. His lazy eye didn't bother her in the least, but the peculiar leather pouch covered in illegible scribbles and hanging from a leather strip about his neck made her skin pucker.

Oliver was right too.

If the man had seen the inside of a bath tub in the past month, she'd lop her hair off. More than a little unsettling to have someone so malodorous preparing their food.

Turning her face into the wind, her twin sighed. "I'm so glad to be out of our stuffy cabin. I pray the weather holds for another week."

Oliver had said they'd entered the Bay of Biscay and should expect the conditions to turn heavy soon, but Blaike hadn't the heart to tell Blaire. Today was her twin's first day above deck. Still pale, and certainly thinner, she didn't need to know her constitution would be tested again. And soon.

"Pretty bubbies," M'Lady Lottie said.

When that didn't earn anything more than a raised brow from either twin, the cockatoo flapped her wings and screamed, "Hopper-arsed whore."

A few sailors chuckled or commented on her latest coarse adage.

Hard to believe they hadn't heard them all before.

Blaire grinned at the cockatoo, now dangling upside down in her cage and playing with a bell. "She certainly is entertaining. Do you think someone actually taught her to say those awful things, or did she learn by overhearing them?"

"I have no idea, but it's not that easy to get her to say new things. I'm trying to teach her a few less unsavory phrases." So far, the effort had proved futile, even when tempting her with cooked beans, which Oliver said were a favorite treat. "She turns her back on me when I try to get her to say, 'Pretty bird.' Instead, she squawks, 'Lady—'"

"Bird." Blaire chuckled while grasping her raspberry colored cloak closed where it gaped slightly at her neck. "I'm fairly certain that's another term for a lightskirt."

"Well, considering where she spent the first several years of her life, I'm not the least surprised."

"Odd that, don't you think? Do you suppose she was a gift from a . . . patron?" Blaire placed a raisin on her gloved palm, then extended it toward the precocious bird. "Me-ow. Me-ow."

"Meow? You want her to meow?" Blaike laughed. "Perchance we can teach her to moo, baa, and oink as well."

Blaire rolled a shoulder. "Any utterance would be an improvement over her current sculduddery." She pushed her hand farther into the cage. "Me-ow. Me-ow."

M'Lady Lottie cocked her head, snatched the raisin with her beak, then swiftly swallowed the fruit.

"You didn't even try to say meow." Blaire leveled the bird a perturbed look.

"Mort. Prime mort. Moooort!" the cockatoo screamed.

"Definitely not a meow," Blaike giggled. "So far I've heard her say trollop, whore, lady bird, and mort." She pushed a strand of hair back beneath her hood. "I blush to think what other terms for ladies of the evening she may suddenly squawk."

They weren't supposed to know about such women. Nevertheless, anyone who'd spent any time in Town attending fashionable assemblies had heard whispers about *those* creatures.

Light skirts, Demimondaines. Lady birds. Bit o' muslins. *Chère-amies.* Cyprians. Courtesans.

My, the *haut ton* certainly had a number of names for the unfortunate women. Perhaps because for all of the upper ten thousands' pretense of propriety, immorality ran rampant among their prestigious, often hypocritical ranks.

How many of those soiled doves had been reduced to that low status through no fault of their own?

Seeking Oliver's familiar form, Blaike scanned the ship's deck. She'd found herself doing that often these past days. Also found herself recalling over and over those final, startling words he'd uttered in his sleep.

Blaike. I love you.

Could it be true?

For a moment, her pulse thrilled at the notion then stuttered to its regular rhythm. If he felt that way, he definitely knew how to hide it.

Never a flirt, and certainly not wanting to appear fast, she'd attempted to subtly let him know she had warm feelings for him, too.

Perhaps not love. Yet.

But definitely something bubbled behind her chest every time he turned those black as molasses eyes on her. Most assuredly the feeling was worth exploring further.

She turned her face toward the billowing sails. There was something majestic and invigorating about being on the open sea. A freedom lacking on land. Which was odd, because a ship more closely confined her.

Oliver said if the winds held, they'd make port early. The news didn't excite her as much as it did her twin. The ocean's swells lifted and lowered the ship, the motion soothing and exhilarating. Blaire wouldn't likely agree with that assessment either.

Trying not to be too obvious, Blaike swept her gaze across the ship once more.

Where was he?

Not a hint in his mannerism or speech suggested he held her in any special regard. Except for that first night when he'd been half-foxed. Even during her two navigation lessons, he'd been as polite and formal as a hired tutor. He'd made sure they were in full view of his crew as he showed her how to use the sextant and never even as much as touched her unless necessary.

In fact, since that first night, he seemed to avoid being alone with her.

Even when she changed his bandage, Hawkins or Webb puttered around the cabin. She might not be an expert at ship hierarchy, but she was fairly certain the first mate and the bosun didn't generally feed birds, clean their cages, make beds, or conduct other trifling duties such as polishing their captain's boots.

The expected invitation to dine with him had not manifested either.

Confound it.

Confound him.

Blaike didn't quite know whether to be miffed or admire him for his diligence in protecting her reputation. Or . . . the unwelcome thought barged into her speculations. Mayhap he wasn't as fascinated with her as she was with him?

Then why would he say something that provocative as he slept?

The unconscious mind was a marvelous thing. It revealed what a person refused to acknowledge when they were awake.

At least that was her unproven theory.

Blaike found herself almost desperate to be alone with Oliver. To recapture that magic of the first night. To encourage his interest. To hear him whisper those lovely, magical words again.

Beyond that, she hadn't considered. For certain, she wasn't about to divulge what he'd muttered in his sleep.

Perhaps he might declare himself before they reached England.

Slow down.

One step at a time.

But time ran short. They'd reach London within a week.

Scrutinizing the decks once more, she saw him disappearing through the companionway.

"Blaire, it's time to change Captain Whitehouse's bandages. Would you like to stay here, since you've been cooped up below for so long?" Touching her sister's shoulder, Blaike smiled. "I know such things make you a bit queasy. I can ask Mr. Hawkins or one of the other officers to keep a watchful eye on you if you are uncomfortable being alone. However, the sailors have been nothing but respectful and helpful to me."

Leaning on the railing, her sister closed her eyes. "I'd rather stay here, if you don't mind. I'm not fond of enclosed spaces, and the odors lingering below make my stomach a bit tetchy. Besides," she angled her head to peer at M'Lady Lottie. "I'm determined to teach her to say something."

Blaike squeezed her sister's fingertips. "I shan't be

above fifteen minutes."

Unless she could tempt Oliver to kiss her.

Oh, now there was a delicious notion.

Precisely how did one go about such things?

Even when motives are pure and
good-intentioned, divulging a secret is
akin to opening Pandora's box. All manner of
complications may arise, so judiciously consider
the consequences before opening your mouth.
~Scruples and Scandals
The Genteel Lady's Guide to Practical Living

12

Oliver winced as he slid a palm inside his shirt
collar.

Sure enough. His fingertips came away damp and
red-tinted.

Confound it.

Served him right for pushing himself too hard too
soon. If Blaike had seen him acting the rigging monkey
to rescue M'Lady Lottie before the twins came up top
today, she'd ring him a peal, to be sure.

After making quick work of removing his coat and
vest, he shucked his shirt. He seldom wore neckcloths
at sea. No society hoity toities aboard the *Sea Gypsy* to
look down their noses at him in condemnation for

forgoing fashion for common sense.

Truth to tell, he only had two neckcloths in decent condition, and those he saved for times when a cravat was required.

Even the coat he donned this morning was for the benefit of the Culpeppers. He usually just captained the ship wearing a shirt, trousers, and boots.

Bright scarlet stained the cloth affixed to his shoulder, and he wrinkled his forehead in frustration as he rummaged through the basket of bandages.

How hard could it be to replace the scrap?

He scowled.

Cutting the bindings circling his ribs and back he could manage, but wrapping new ones might prove tricky.

Hawkins should be along any moment to discuss tonight's activities. Care needed to be taken that none of the men overindulged, and monitoring the crew fell to the first mate. Especially since the clouds on the horizon portended what could become a nasty squall.

Oliver had plotted a course that should keep them ahead of the tempest; if the wind held, that was. But at sea, as he'd learned a long time ago, nothing was guaranteed. Far wiser to always assume the worst and take precautions.

Hawkins would advise divine entreaties, but prayer without a plan seemed foolish.

Oliver glared at the linens binding him. His first mate could be pressed into lending a hand with the bandage, though he was as worthless as Oliver with this sort of thing.

Scissors in hand he stood before his washstand. He tilted the mirror to better see his wound and had just slipped one blade under the strips below his arm when a knock rattled his stateroom door.

"Come."

As usual, Hawkins's timing was impeccable. What would he do without the man?

Neck bent to see his handiwork, Oliver clamped his teeth against the shooting pain and edged the blades farther under the bands.

"Just what do you think you're doing?"

Blaike.

He started and jabbed the blade into his ribs.

"Ouch, blast it! I nearly impaled myself." Withdrawing the scissors, he sent her a frustrated scowl. "What are *you* doing?"

"Your dressing should've been changed hours ago." Her lovely eyes grew round as groats as she raked him with her reproachful gaze, then they narrowed to accusatory slits. "Oh, Oliver. You're bleeding again. What have you been doing?"

She hurried to him, unclasping her cloak as she flew across his quarters. After draping her wrap over his desk chair, she pushed her sleeves to her elbows.

"How did this happen? Your wound has been healing so well." She pulled her mouth taut. "At least I thought it was. Perhaps I should've sutured it after all. Or cauterized it. That book," she pointed to the thick, russet leather volume on the corner of his desk, "recommends doing so to stop bleeding."

Doubt shadowed the gaze she lifted to meet his.

"The fault isn't yours, Blaike. It's mine. A captain's duties are often rigorous."

And he'd have to be on his deathbed to permit a fire-heated blade to sear his flesh.

She needn't know he'd climbed the rat lines earlier to rescue an enraged bird screaming, "Bums and bubbies" and "fusty luggs," as the *Sea Gypsy's* crew hooted and guffawed below.

At least M'Lady Lottie provided a welcome distraction for the men.

"It's a good thing I followed you." Pointing to the bed, she took the scissors from him, her gaze lingering a trifle overly-long on his hairy chest. "Sit down, please."

Oliver obeyed, leaning back on his hands, and tracking her graceful movements. He'd never tire of that. Or hearing her voice. Or her laughter.

Acutely conscious of his nakedness, for an instant, he considered how he might partially cover himself. He pitched the notion aside almost immediately.

Blaike wouldn't be able to tend to her ministrations if he did.

She'd seen his chest numerous times over the past few days, but there'd always been someone else present to make the situation more respectable. And less torturous for the carnal cravings he must deny. Far too tempting to have her touching him when, with every pore, every nerve, he longed to take her in his arms and kiss her luscious lips until they both gasped.

In fact, he'd like to kiss every part of her, starting with her bowed mouth and ending with her dainty toes, worshipping every curve in between.

Concentrate on something else.

Not the sweet essence wafting from her pearly skin.

"Do you want a dram of brandy or whisky first?" Blaike asked, bending over him. "We'll call it an early beginning to your birthday celebration."

She gave him a playful smile, that familiar mischievous light glinting in her arresting blue eyes.

Was she flirting?

If only he had the right to encourage her. To declare himself. To utter the words tapping at the back of his teeth.

"Oliver? Do you want a drink?"

The question tore him from his reverie.

"No," he managed while slanting his head to better

smell her hair.

Sunlight and blossoms. And Blaike.

If he lived to be a one-hundred year old curmudgeon, he'd never forget her scent. Or the feeling of contentment and completion it roused in him. They were embedded upon his memory, entrenched in his emotions, for all time.

"I never partake when I know the crew will imbibe." A wise captain didn't indulge when his crew celebrated, particularly with a storm bearing down upon them. As it was, he'd have to limit their festivities. They'd not grumble overly much, for the men also knew the dangers of underestimating the fickle weather or the equally capricious ocean.

"The bleeding has stopped, but I want to sterilize the wound again." Her pretty face pinched in concentration, she gingerly snipped the bands from beneath both of his arms. "It will burn something fierce, I'm afraid."

Definitely don't think of the tempting handfuls mere inches away and pressing against her simple blue gown.

A gown that allowed the slightest alluring view of the satiny mounds the bodice caressed.

Damned lucky fabric.

He groaned, and not from the slight tugging of his shoulder as she drew the strips away.

"I'm sorry." One long-fingered hand resting on his good shoulder, she glanced up, her eyes brimming with sympathy. "Am I hurting you?"

Yes. His manhood twitched an answer.

His aching heart pinged in agreement. *Aye.*

"I'm fine. Just hurry and rewrap it. I have things to do." His response came out much terser than he'd intended.

Blaike quickly lowered her lashes, surprisingly dark given her pale hair and brows, but not before he saw the hurt and disappointment his sharp retort caused.

After cleansing the gouge, she laid a fresh square on it, and with practiced ease, rewrapped his shoulder. Dismay radiated from her, silent yet potent, as she worked.

"Forgive me, *cara.*" Though he knew he shouldn't, he caressed her satiny cheek. "I'm angry at myself, not you."

Angry that he couldn't control his feelings toward her, physical or emotional.

Angry that they lived in such an unjust world that he would never be able to declare himself.

Angry that she could never be his.

Angry that he'd have to hurt this wondrous woman. That he'd have to watch the affection glistening in her glorious eyes fade, then die when they reached London, and he delivered her to her family without a backward glance or a word of farewell.

Lest on that day, she see his desolation and realize the colossal untruth he professed when he told her she meant nothing to him.

Blaike slowly lifted her lashes, and what shined in the depths of her eyes caused Oliver's heart to stop for an instant, then resume beating with the force of a winded racehorse.

She wanted him, too.

God curse him for a fool, but he wrapped his other arm around her trim waist, ignoring the angry stab of pain it caused his injury. He drew her, unresisting, between his thighs, then ever so gradually, slid his hand over the nape of her neck and urged her nearer so that their mouths touched.

Flames burst behind his eyelids and passion streaked through him as wild and uncontrolled as if someone had touched a spark to black powder, igniting a firestorm.

Blaike made a throaty, hungry noise and edged nearer, her thigh bumping his length and sending his lust spiraling ever higher.

What he'd meant as a tender brush of lips to comfort and reassure her, a swift stolen taste of her honeyed mouth, exploded into desire so strong, his head spun.

Palms splayed, he held her, his tongue teasing her

plump lower lip until her mouth parted.

Her hand on his shoulder flexed then clenched. Snaking the fingers of her other hand into his hair, she angled her head to permit him deeper access.

No timid, shy miss here, but a woman who gave as much as she took.

Inexperienced and a trifle clumsy at first, she learned the art of kissing with prodigious aptitude.

"Oliver," she moaned, arching into him.

Never had hearing his name sounded so seductive.

Kicking his chiding conscience, as well as his once noble intentions overboard, he clasped Blaike to his chest and lay back on the bed, taking her with him.

The ropes supporting the mattress squeaked as their weight jarred the bed.

"Your shoulder," she gasped, settling atop him.

"Will be fine," he murmured against her mouth, while daring to squeeze the luscious mounds of her behind. "*Ti adoro.*"

He did adore her.

She sank into his chest, their legs and tongues entangling.

The pain in his shoulder paled in comparison to the burning passion for the woman in his arms.

He'd regret this.

Aye, but he'd also treasure this precious encounter for the remainder of his days.

How often had he imagined kissing her sweet mouth? Those dewy, pink lips? Wondered what it would be like to hold her svelte form in his arms? To have her melt into him with a woman's desire as she did now?

'Twas more profound and soul shattering than he'd dreamed.

He'd known to yield to this mad urge was foolhardy and reckless. Knew deep in the recesses of his spirit, he'd never be satisfied or content with mere kissing. Recognized on a primitive level that no other female would ever make him feel this way. That he'd never want another woman with such desperate intensity after her.

He loved her.

Sei la mia anima gemella.

Blaike *was* his soulmate. He'd guessed it from the beginning but had denied the probability.

"Mmm, you smell good. Like your coffee. Spicy and," she sniffed his neck, "maybe a hint of cedar too. Very manly."

God help him.

She framed his face with her hands, raining hot, moist kisses over his face and jaw. Rubbing her satiny cheek against his, she released a soft sigh. "I adore your beard."

Was that sultry siren's voice his Blaike's?

She ran her long fingers down his torso, then spread them through the hair on his chest, gently tugging.

The sensation had him on the cusp of spilling into his trousers.

"I've wanted to do this since I first saw you shirtless."

His muscles quivered and jumped in eager response to her exploration.

"And I've wanted to kiss you since I first laid eyes on you," Oliver confessed.

Stupid to reveal that. It hinted at something that could never be.

"And you waited this long?" The smile curving her mouth held more than delight. It revealed a woman's promise. "I'm not sure if I'm flattered or peeved."

He was a selfish arse, for he reveled in the knowledge despite the impropriety.

She feathered her hand down the narrow track of hair that disappeared into his waistband, then boldly looking him in the eye, slipped her fingers beneath the fabric.

Her smile—sexy, wanton, and willing—almost had him tearing open his trousers' falls, hoisting her skirts, and seizing the bliss coupling with her would bring them both.

Instead, Oliver grabbed her hand.

"Blaike, Stop. You don't know what you're doing."

"Of course I do." A suggestive half-smile tipping her mouth, she arched a brow. "Have you forgotten, I was raised on a dairy farm? I know full well what happens between the sexes. The act doesn't frighten me, though I believe males mount from behind don't they?"

Such a matter of fact question. She wasn't the least bit embarrassed or shy. Just curious, adorably naïve, and brazen.

Face crumpled in puzzlement, she eyed his groin. "I need to be on my hands and knees, don't I?"

Yes, by Poseidon.

On her knees. Her back. Her incredibly long legs about his waist. Straddling him. Over his desk. Sitting. Standing . . .

With her firm, alabaster breasts pressed to his chest, practically spilling from her bodice, Oliver was pressed almost beyond control to resist her innocent invitation.

Except a woman like Blaike expected marriage.

Deserved marriage.

Her family would demand a union if he selfishly took what she so generously offered. If Ravensdale or Leventhorpe didn't have him keel-hauled, drawn and quartered, or challenge him to a duel. Blaike merited more than a hurried tumble or the modest, often difficult, life of a sailor's wife. For if Oliver couldn't convince Longhurst to accept a partial payment, the *Sea Gypsy*—*home for almost fifteen years*—was lost to him.

He had friends and family who would lend him funds. As much as he required, truth be known.

No.

If he succeeded in extracting himself from the gutter he'd been born into, he'd do so on his own. No one else would be able to take any measure of credit.

That was why Oliver had never planned on marrying. He must be faithful to the sea, for she'd given him his start. He'd never contemplated anything else. Didn't know how to do anything else. The sea had always been, would always be his future.

Not the aroused vixen in his bed, as much as Oliver might wish it otherwise.

If naught else, he was a pragmatic man. Life's realities had taught him not to put store or hope in things unseen. In what-ifs and maybes. Which, as much as it troubled Hawkins, was why Oliver couldn't share his first-mate's faith in an all-knowing deity.

Besides, Blaike's sister and cousins had all married well. Made brilliant matches, truth to tell. Each married to a lord of the realm.

She could, too, someday.

If he stayed away.

Her fascination would fade in time. She'd

recognize her infatuation for what it was: confused gratitude brought about because he'd plucked her from Abraham's clutches.

What driveling rot, his cynical conscience scoffed.

Blast it all. At times, Oliver truly detested his integrity.

Still, he must refuse that which he wanted most. That which would make Blaike his until death separated them. That which might assure his happiness, but at the expense of hers.

Closing his eyes and clamping his jaw, he clutched her exploring hands.

"*Dolcezza,* sweetheart, we must stop before we're discovered. I shan't have you compromised because of me." He sat up, gritting his teeth against the agony now stabbing his shoulder. "I thought you were Hawkins when I bid you enter. He's expected any moment."

Her eyes widened as chagrin tightened her features.

"Why didn't you say so earlier? We might have been interrupted."

Blaike jumped from the bed.

Adjusting her clothing, she rushed to the washstand where she smoothed her hair, darting confused glances at Oliver in the looking glass. She mightn't be experienced in passion, but she'd recognized his desire.

Silent since she'd leaped from his bed, she tidied

the medicine basket, then gathered the soiled cloths and dropped them in the washstand basin.

Just as silent, he donned a fresh shirt, then shrugged into his coat.

Noisy footsteps, more like stomping, echoed outside Oliver's quarters, along with a warbling whistle. That, too, seemed rather loud and contrived. A couple of times, someone bumped the passageway bulkhead—hard—then hollered a cheerful greeting. Either the fellow was half-soused already or deliberately making his presence known.

Hawkins.

Subtle as a hippopotamus in a ballroom.

Blaike didn't seem to notice. She'd moved to his desk and picked up the volume he'd been reading. Or at least tried to read. He found *Gulliver's Travels* more vexing than entertaining.

Perchance, the recurring thoughts of Blaike interrupting his reading might be more to blame than the novel.

"You and your sister are welcome to any of the books in my library." Not extensive to be sure, nonetheless, the built in bookshelf below the windows held two-score volumes. "I have decks of cards and a chess board, too."

"Oh, thank you. I'm sure she'll be as eager as I am

to accept your offer."

Her enthusiasm didn't reflect in her eyes. She'd rather he gave her more lessons in navigation and astronomy, he'd be bound.

Oliver despised the uncertainty he read in Blaike's posture and expression. And damn his eyes, he couldn't, didn't dare, reassure her.

His love *must* remain a secret.

Theirs wasn't a misunderstanding that a simple conversation would solve. Perhaps in gothic tales, true love endured whilst the characters lived in poverty, content with nothing more than their lover's company. But such was fanciful fluff. Ridiculed and shunned, hungry, cold, and perhaps even ill. Those as well as other hardships would chink away at love until nothing remained but disillusionment and resentment.

Call him a coward, but he couldn't bear to have Blaike gaze at him with disenchantment, scorn, or bitterness.

Three sharp raps preceded Hawkins calling, "Cap'n? I need a moment."

Oliver finished securing his hair, for to leave it down would surely raise his mate's suspicion. Not a gossip by any means, Hawkins was more apt to lecture Oliver on moral failings if he suspected anything had occurred.

"Come."

At once the door swung open, and the first mate shuffled inside, nodding a greeting. "Miss. Sir."

Oliver didn't miss the swift, assessing glance Hawkins sent Blaike. He could expect a sermon later. He'd stake his reputation on it.

"I'll join my sister." Blaike swung her cloak about her shoulders. "I've left Blaire alone far longer than I anticipated. Oliver, do try to refrain from opening your wound again." She glanced out the window, furrows creasing her forehead as she secured the frogs at her throat. "Those clouds don't look friendly."

"I think if we stay our course, we'll run ahead of the storm." Oliver couldn't be positive, naturally. He tentatively flexed his shoulder, hating the stiffness that limited his movements.

"What was it you needed, Hawkins?"

"A sail's been sighted a fair distance off."

Not unusual by any means.

However, what Hawkins *wasn't* saying sent alarm tingling the length of Oliver's spine.

He cut Blaike a troubled glance. "Why don't you go topside and see how your sister fares?"

His men wouldn't conceive of touching either woman, but Blaire didn't know that, this being her first day topside.

"Not until you tell me why Mr. Hawkins's face looks like a goose's back end." Blaike folded her arms. A Mother Superior's acrid glance held less starch or challenge.

Too smart, his Blaike.

Jaw unhinged at her comparison, Hawkins swung a desperate glance to Oliver.

Rubbing his temple, Oliver shrugged. "She'll know soon enough. Give over. What has you wearing such a Friday face?"

"She's pacing us, and she's not flying any colors, Cap'n."

When deciding whether to disclose a
secret, a far-sighted woman considers who
might most benefit and who will be most harmed.
~Scruples and Scandals
The Genteel Lady's Guide to Practical Living

13

Friend or foe?

Blaike peered at the horizon, striving to catch a glimpse of the ship Hawkins said was out there, somewhere off the *Sea Gypsy's* starboard side. Though she trusted Oliver completely, trepidation nevertheless padded across her shoulders.

If friendly, why hadn't the vessel struck her colors?

Maybe ships only did so under certain circumstances.

What type of vessel pursued them?

A pirate ship?

Captain Abraham?

Could the *Sea Gypsy* outrun her if need be?

She was a sleek clipper, but could a larger ship overtake her? Blaike's knowledge of mariner protocol wouldn't fill an infant's shoe.

At the helm, Oliver conversed in low tones with Mr. Grover, Mr. Hawkins, and a couple of other officers. None appeared particularly harrowed or concerned. No doubt, these situations were common enough and seasoned seamen took the occurrences in their stride.

She wasn't altogether sure she ever could.

Swinging her attention the port side, she pinched her lips together.

Sullen charcoal-colored clouds billowed low over the rolling, white-capped waves. Possible danger lurked on either side of the grayish-green waters as night enshrouded the vessel.

Even the air smelled and felt different: a sweet, pungent scent that tickled her nostrils and heightened her awareness whilst making her prickly all over.

Oliver had directed the helmsmen to stay the course, right between the two potential threats. He'd even ordered the galley stove extinguished, and at this moment, the crew was stowing away or lashing down anything that might be tossed about in rough seas.

Or in a battle?

The *Sea Gypsy* had but one gun deck as well as a chase gun on the bow and stern. She wasn't designed for lengthy fighting.

Cold sweat dampened Blaike's underarms, and a peculiar metallic taste filled her mouth. She'd been afraid before, had been terrified when Captain Abraham said he intended to sell her into sexual slavery. But she'd never tasted this kind of fear. Nor smelled it before either, yet she kept catching whiffs of an unsettling, acerbic aroma.

"Blaike, why has Captain Whitehouse cancelled tonight's celebration? And why is the crew scurrying about like squirrels preparing for winter?"

Blaire touched Blaike's forearm, two neat rows wrinkling her forehead.

What to say to not worry her further?

Might as well tell her the whole truth. Intelligent as she was, she'd soon figure it out for herself.

"A storm brews, and another ship's sails were sighted earlier. We don't know if the vessel is friendly." Blaike summoned a cheery smile, which quickly slid into a compassionate curve of her mouth at her twin's distraught sound.

"I confess, I'm not made for seafaring." Features strained, Blaire hunched deeper into her cloak. "I rather dislike everything about it."

No doubt the prospect of angry, roiling seas caused her distress, making Blaike all the more grateful she didn't suffer from seasickness. She'd seen the havoc the condition wreaked upon her twin and worried for her health.

"Don't fret, dearest. Oliver says he thinks we'll stay ahead of the storm, but he's taking precautions just in case."

"Doodle sack."

The wind carried M'Lady Lottie's latest crudity to where Blaike stood, one hand resting on the smooth rail.

Locked in her cage, she voiced her annoyance at being confined.

Would Oliver secure her below until the threats had passed?

"Blaike! Look." Her voice thick with dread, Blaire shook Blaike's shoulder.

Twisting to look where her twin pointed, Blaike's lungs constricted as her heart seemed to swell to twice its normal size behind her breastbone.

The ship she'd strained to see had emerged from twilight's nebulous glow, a large black silhouette on the seascape.

How had she gained on them so quickly?

Why would she if she meant the *Sea Gypsy* no harm?

What if the occupants needed help, though?

Wouldn't they have given a distress signal then?

A fat raindrop splattered onto her nose as she threw

a glance over her shoulder.

Oliver, his strong legs spread, held a brass spyglass to his eye, as did Mr. Hawkins, both directed at the looming vessel. Even from where she stood, the grim line of his mouth and the harsh planes of his face were visible.

If her stomach hadn't already been a gnarled knot of anxiety, it would've turned to stone.

Her worry wasn't for herself.

As captain, Oliver was at greatest risk if an unfriendly vessel overtook and boarded them.

The eyeglass still held in place, he said something to his first mate, and with a sharp nod, Mr. Hawkins sprinted into action.

"All hands on deck," he bellowed. For such a small man, he possessed an impressive shout.

Foe then.

Fright's sharp claws scraped along Blaike's nerves.

The *Sea Gypsy* swung to port, facing into the gale.

"Oh, this isn't good, is it?" Blaire grasped Blaike's hand. "I may cast up my accounts right here."

"Take deep breaths, and try to stay calm. Look at the horizon" Sound advice if a potential enemy's ship didn't hover there. Even Blaike's robust constitution wobbled a mite. "I trust Oliver. He knows what he's about."

She did trust him, but sailing directly into a tempest meant that tactic was less dangerous than engaging the ship swooping down upon them.

Cold, heavy pellets fell faster from the sky, even as the wind tore Blaike's hood off.

"Misses, you'll need to go below now."

Mr. Grover touched his hat, his countenance taut with tension.

"Cap'n's orders. And there'll be no hot meals served until further notice. Someone will deliver hardtack, water, dried apples, and cheese to your quarters when they're able. The Cap'n also doesn't want any unnecessary lamps burning. Once you're in your cabin, you must remain inside until advised otherwise. The passageways won't be lit, and with the ship bobbing about, it'd be dangerous not to stay put. "

Bobbing? This was dashed more than bobbing.

"We understand." Blaike cast a fretful glance toward the wicked clouds.

They'd be stuck in the ship's bowels with no light and roiling on the mountainous waves.

For how long? Hours? Days?

Blaike looped arms with Blaire, now as pale as the sheets billowing from the masts above.

"I vow, after this, I'm never setting foot on a ship again." A hand pressed to her throat, Blaire swallowed.

Sailors scrambled up the rigging and rat lines, hollering to one another. Howling wind and crashing waves muted their call. Brave and daring at any time, in this weather, their actions were positively heroic. Likely an absolute necessity, too.

"At once, if you please, Misses."

Probably a dozen things requiring his attention, Mr. Grover hurried away.

Even as Blaike and her sister cautiously made their way across the deck, the wind whipped into a frenzy, lashing her face with icy, bean-sized drops. The raw force of nature was something to behold. At once glorious and terrifying. Candescent purplish-white lightening branches rent the distant sky, followed by muffled explosions of thunder.

"A moment, please." Striding to the companionway, M'Lady Lottie clinging to his hand, Oliver addressed them both, but looked at Blaike. "Can I impose upon you to take her to my quarters, and put her in her cage? She has food and water enough to last a couple of days. I don't know when I'll be able to get below again."

Extending her arm, Blaike nodded. "Of course."

"Bedded and buggered," the cockatoo said, except she lacked her usual ornery attitude.

"Are we actually sailing into that?" Blaike tilted her

head at the ominous mass as he transferred the disgruntled bird to her.

"No." The wind had torn his hair free, and it hung in saturated tendrils to his shoulders. "That would be suicide. I'm using the squall's perimeter as a shield. Night will be fully upon us within the hour. I intend to use them both to mask us from the other vessel, which I'm sure you've seen."

"Do you know who the other ship is?" She accepted the cockatoo, surprised at how heavy the bird was.

He nodded, shoving a hank of hair from his eyes.

"I do, and we don't wish to encounter them. Which is why I've chosen this course. The *Sea Gypsy's* cargo will act as a ballast, and I'm veering her into an area with the shallowest waves and lowest winds. I've also given the order to periodically dump a gallon or two of oil to calm the waves for us. Not too much though, else the other ship will spot us or benefit from the oil."

Blaike couldn't form the words burning on the tip of her tongue. Perchance, she didn't really want to know what he so obviously withheld.

Just who was pursuing them?

Maybe the gallivanting around the high seas with Oliver wasn't such a cheery prospect after all. There was something to be said for boring and safe.

And solid, unmoving land.

Without pirates or other scallywags.

"Blaike, I'm not feeling at all well. If you don't mind, I'll go to our cabin straightaway and lie down."

If Blaire felt this miserable already, Blaike dreaded what the next few hours would bring. Her twin truly might very well never sail again. Even Blaike's tummy protested the merest bit at the ship's increased churning.

"Yes, go along, dear. I'll be there just a soon as I've dealt with M'Lady Lottie."

Summoning a weak, closed-mouth smile, Blaire descended the ladder.

Blaike touched Oliver's wound, then searched his eyes. "You will be careful, won't you? Promise me? I'll fret until I see you safe again."

Bold of her, but what if something happened to him?

She wanted him to know she cared, even if now wasn't the time to declare her affection.

Angling his back, partially sheltering her from the furious elements, and likely the crew's regard as well, he grazed her cheek with his rough thumb.

"I promise. But you must make me the same promise, *cara. Sei tutto per me.*"

The ship heeled violently to starboard, and he stumbled into her.

M'Lady Lottie screeched her outrage, digging her

claws into Blaike's fingers. "Bawdy baskets."

Blaike didn't even want to guess what bawdy baskets were.

For certain, something that would turn her cheeks pink.

"I must go. Get below, *cara*."

Oliver kissed her forehead, the act so endearing and natural, she couldn't object.

Had no inclination to.

She clutched his soggy shirtfront with her free hand.

"Wait, Oliver. What does it mean? What you just said to me in Italian?"

He winked, a roguish twinkle in his eye and looking every bit the rakish pirate she'd likened him to be those many months ago. "That's my secret."

"Oliver. That's not—"

The *Sea Gypsy* crested another gigantic wave, hurtling them into the companionway.

Pain ratcheted from shoulder to hip, and she gasped. Still, he wasn't getting off so easily. Clutching his sodden shirt, she shook it.

"What does it mean, you stubborn man?"

"Cap'n!" Such urgency filled Hawkins' voice, her blood congealed in her veins.

"It means, you are everything to me, *amore mia*."

After casting a grim look behind him, Oliver gave her a firm push. "Go. Now. I cannot have you distracting me, and if you're up here, I shan't be able to concentrate on anything but your safety. Pray we survive the next few hours and lose the other vessel."

What fool would try to overtake a ship on the cusp of a gale?

Over his shoulder, the outline of sails obstructed the angry horizon.

That one, whoever the lunatic captain might be.

Stifling another gasp, Blaike clambered down the ladder, no easy feat, wearing long skirts and with a frightened bird bobbing and swaying.

And swearing.

Thrice, M'Lady Lottie's wings battered her face.

A single lamp hanging near the ladder lit the passageway. How soon before it was extinguished?

Minutes likely.

She must hurry, not at all certain she could find her way to her cabin in a pitch black passageway.

"Lottie scared. Hurry. Hurry." Her agitation growing, M'Lady Lottie chattered non-stop. "Hurry. Dunnock doxy. Bushel bubby. I'm scared. Petey? Hell's bells. Limp as lace."

"*Shh*, Lottie. I cannot think with you blathering."

Had Blaire made it to their cabin all right?

She'd looked positively green around her mouth, and panic had glinted in her eyes. Probably afraid she was about to cast her crumpets in view of all. Mayhap another slop bucket would be a good idea. But where to get one amidst this chaos?

If they'd been permitted light, Blaike would borrow the medical journal and research how to treat seasickness other than ginger tea. Though Fairnly had prepared several cups a day for her sister, the brew didn't help appease her nausea.

Why she was so afflicted, yet Blaike barely so didn't make any sense at all. They were so similar— identical—in almost every other way.

"Petey? Ol-eeve? Lottie afraid."

Poor Lottie. She wanted her owner to comfort her.

"I know, Lottie. It's all right. I'll take care of you."

Holding the terrified bird close to her midriff, Blaike ran a soothing hand down the cockatoo's back.

As Blaike jostled down the ever increasing dimmer passageway to Oliver's quarters, bouncing from bulkhead to bulkhead as she trundled along, M'Lady Lottie tottered on her fingers. Amazing the sheer strength of the bird's feet.

She bustled into the great cabin. Mindful of the rows of windows and what Mr. Grover had said about lighting lamps, she left the door open. The dim passageway light barely sufficed to illuminate the chamber.

Nonetheless, Blaike had been inside so many times, she easily made her way to M'Lady Lottie's cage, only banging her shin once on the trunk usually situated at the foot of Oliver's bed.

She squinted round the cabin. Most furnishings were fixed to the deck, but those that weren't had shifted. Like the chest, now in the middle of the cabin, as well as any unsecured items from atop his desk.

"There you are." She rested her hand against the wooded dowel, and the cockatoo shimmied onto her perch. "I know you don't like your cage, but it's for your own safety."

"Randy rantallion," the bird muttered peevishly as Blaike latched the door.

"I'm positive I don't want to know what that is."

Shaking her head, she shivered, soaked to the skin. She didn't relish trying to change into a dry gown and chemise in the dark.

"From your lively discourses, Lottie, I'm beginning to presume women of low virtue also have tetchy dispositions."

A monstrous wave battered the sturdy vessel, rattling the windows and banging the door shut. Blaike stumbled sideways, crashing into the washstand. A moment later, the ship pitched hard to port, and she was thrown to the deck. Her right knee, hip, and shoulder collided with the unforgiving wood, and she yelped as piercing pain speared her.

M'Lady screamed in alarm, flying around her cage in terror. "Hell's bells. Devil's at the door."

An occasional shout could be heard above the furor and the vessel's anguished creaks and groans as the gale pummeled the ship.

A book skidded across the floor and *thunked* into the bulkhead.

This was the squall's fringe?

The *Sea Gypsy* bobbled about like an acorn below a waterwheel.

Blaike rolled over, and breathing heavily, assessed her injuries. Cautious and tentative, she flexed and stretched. Nothing appeared broken, but her knee and shoulder ached something awful. If these were the shallowest waves, she never wanted to experience anything worse.

That notion of sailing round the world could bugger itself.

Pray God Blaire had wedged herself in her berth. She was likely terrified.

All the more reason why Blaike must get to her twin.

Eyes squeezed shut, and jaw clenched against an unladylike oath, she sat up. With a groan, she shoved to her feet, then hands held before her, shuffled toward where she thought the door ought to be.

The *Sea Gypsy* rolled again, diving into a trough between the towering walls of water.

The abrupt motion launched Blaike forward into the trunk. She cried out as her knees connected with the unyielding chest, and again as she toppled to the side, smashing her head against the bed.

'Tis a simple, but profound secret,
and one a charitable woman heeds:
Everything worth doing, is what is done for
others without regard or expectation of recompense.
~*Scruples and Scandals*
The Genteel Lady's Guide to Practical Living

14

Two days later, the first metallic traces of dawn feathered the sky as Oliver trained his spyglass across the gold, copper, and bronze seascape. No more worrying about being sent arse over chin into the fitful ocean now that the wind had abated to a peevish breeze.

The worrisome Bay of Biscay lay behind them and England ahead.

A modicum of tension eased from his shoulders, and he rubbed his nape. His gamble, the riskiest and with the highest stakes he'd ever wagered, had paid off.

With a practiced eye, he scrutinized the ocean one final time.

Not a sign anywhere of the *Black Dove*.

Despite being a motley lot, he wouldn't wish the

Black Dove's hands to a watery grave—except for Abraham.

That assling deserved to rot in Davy Jones's Locker.

Oliver couldn't summon a jot of forgiveness for him.

Nevertheless, if the *Black Dove* had sustained damage enough to keep them well away from the *Sea Gypsy,* he, too, might offer a prayer of thanksgiving as Hawkins had repeatedly these past few hours.

One had to admire his first mate's faith, even if he didn't understand it.

On either side of Oliver, Hawkins and Grover also perused the ocean with their spyglasses. The sun edged higher on the horizon, spreading her warmth and vibrant hues over the mild swells.

"No sign of another sail, Cap'n, nor a suspicious cloud overhead." Hawkins grinned before angling his gaze skyward and silently acknowledging his God. Again. "I know it ain't right, and I'll have to repent, but I sincerely hope that bleedin' son of a barnacle's bum met his maker. If so, hell's fires are burnin' hotter, for certain."

Oliver and Grover exchanged amused glances.

Make that thrice Hawkins had sworn in front of Oliver.

They closed their spyglasses, the sounds of the brass cylinders sliding shut a satisfying reminder they'd survived the nerve-racking ordeal.

Only just.

"Well done you, sir." Grover shook Oliver's hand. "I confess, yesterday I had my doubts we'd escape that witch's squall. Made me wish I had Hawkins's strong faith, it did."

"With a lesser crew, we wouldn't have done. I commend you all," Oliver said.

He would've like to have offered his men a bonus, but given the cargo holds had room to spare, he didn't dare make such a generous offer. He might just ask Ravensdale a question or two about that shipping heiress. Perhaps she had need of another clipper to transport her goods.

Nonetheless, pride squared his shoulders the merest bit.

Not only had they evaded Abraham, they'd make England day after tomorrow, days ahead of schedule.

Bitter-sweet, that.

Only one more sunrise with Blaike.

A morning months ago at Leventhorpe's country house, sprang to mind. Oliver had suggested she ought to see a sunrise from the deck of a ship.

Even then, she'd enchanted him.

Still, he must let her go. He must.

Grateful that Blaike had obeyed him, he'd neither seen nor heard from her since ordering the twins below. M'Lady Lottie had been curiously silent as well.

The storm and the threat from another vessel served as vivid reminders why he couldn't ask Blaike to remain aboard the *Sea Gypsy*. Last night, missing her horribly though she was safe within the bowels of his ship, he'd entertained that ludicrous notion for all of thirty seconds before reality clobbered him.

Actually, it had been a bucket hurtling across the deck, and plowing into his shoulder blade that brought home the truth.

With painful and undeniable clarity.

Water and oil didn't mix.

Residents of Mayfair's mansions and Whitechapel's slums didn't hobnob together.

Pockets-to-let commoners didn't consort with the gently bred. Such were life's inarguable facts.

The queer pull behind his ribs twitched again, as it did each time he faced that undisputable truth.

For a time that first night, he fretted he'd miscalculated and ventured too near the squall, and the *Sea Gypsy* and all aboard her might be lost. Nevertheless, setting any course that would've permitted Abraham the opportunity to overtake them had been inconceivable. Better the twins should drown than endure what he intended for them.

Bloody exhausted—the only crew member to not have caught a few moments of rest—Oliver yawned, wide and gusty. He needed sleep before he dozed off whilst standing and toppled into the sea.

"Hawkins, you're in command. I'm to bed for a few hours, but I'd like a bath first. Also, have one of the men inform the Culpeppers that they may leave their cabin. In fact, order them baths, as well. We've water enough for certain now, and I'm sure they'd enjoy the luxury."

He clapped his first mate's boney shoulder.

"Fairnly is to outdo himself today. I want hot food for everyone, and lots of it. Simple fare is fine. Salt-pork, beans, potatoes. The men have earned a reward, so they're to have an extra ration of rum as well. If he balks, tell him he hasn't had to earn his way these past two days. Allow him to choose a couple of men to assist him. And please send someone below to bring M'Lady Lottie up. She won't let me sleep a wink if she remains in my quarters."

"Aye. I'll see to it all." A grin still etched upon his weathered face, Hawkins swaggered away whistling his usual hymn, only pausing in his warbling to give orders to a couple of sailors.

Oliver would have liked to personally see how

Blaike had fared, but he hadn't asked for a bath because he longed for a hot soak. He stank of sweat and sea. Fear too, if he were wholly honest with himself. Mayhap he'd check on her after he'd washed.

Just to make sure she was all right.

To see if she *and* her sister needed anything.

Then he could relax and close his gritty, leaden eyes.

Yawning again, he strode to the companionway, taking time to thank and compliment his men as he went. Truly, they'd performed magnificently, and he couldn't be prouder.

He'd already shrugged out of his stiff coat and was unbuckling his belt when he made his quarters.

Lottie's mutters and titters carried to him in the passageway. She'd kick up a dust when she saw him, for certain.

Bracing himself for her loud welcome, he stepped across the threshold and was brought up short.

Blaike sat at his desk, reading a book, the cockatoo perched behind her on the chair's back. A lock of Blaike's unbound hair clenched in her foot, Lottie plucked at the shimmering strand with her beak.

The bird spied him and shrieked, "Ol-eeve! Hello Luv." She swayed back and forth, back and forth, cooing, "Luv Ol-eeve. Missed Ol-eeve."

He couldn't help but chuckle at her exuberant greeting. "Hello, Lottie. How are you?"

"How are you?" she mimicked. "Tired as a trull."

There was the Lottie he'd expected.

"Hello, Blaike."

Nowhere near the words Oliver wanted to say.

I was terrified for you.

I feared the ship was lost, and I'd never see or speak to you again.

I wish life was fair, and I dared to offer for you.

I love you. Senza di te non sono niente.

Without you I am nothing

"Hello, Oliver."

Blaike slowly stood and offered him an almost shy smile. Attired in a serviceable slate gray gown, she'd never appeared lovelier to his hungry gaze.

"I came to feed Lottie. I felt so sorry for her, I let her out for a few minutes again. I hope you don't mind. I'm still trying to teach her new words, too. She's nearly got pretty bird."

She pushed her hair behind her shoulders, and the brilliant mass tumbled to her firm derriere.

Mamma's combs would look stunning in her hair.

As Blaike moved across the cabin, the rising sun's rays burst in, illuminating her countenance—horribly swollen and bruised on the right side.

"My God, *cara mia*. What happened to your face?" Oliver dumped his possessions on his chest as he rushed to her.

For once, Lottie didn't offer a raunchy response. Rather, she flew to his bed and proceeded to parade up and down the counterpane, chattering away in cockatoo.

"I tripped over your trunk that first night. Actually, I was thrown and struck the foot of your bed." Blaike gingerly touched her head. "The cut isn't very big, but I cannot put my hair up. It hurts to twist and pin it."

"Purdy birrr-dy. Purdy birrr-dy," Lottie muttered, testing the new words. "Lottie purdy birrr-dy."

"*Mia cara,* I'm so sorry.

Despite reeking like a London beggar, Oliver pulled her into his embrace, cradling her as if she were the frailest of flowers. Her hair, a shiny curtain, trailed over his arms. Floral and vanilla essences wafted upward from the long tresses.

A whorl of emotion constricted his throat, and he had to swallow twice to dislodge the lump.

Blaike might've been killed. Or lain in his cabin injured and suffering these past two days, and no one would've known, save her sister. And the twin was too ill to move, let alone venture to his quarters.

Guilt and remorse burrowed through him, leaving him raw.

"I should've seen you safely to your cabin. Should never have asked you to take Lottie below."

Tilting her head, Blaike peered into his eyes. "Nonsense. You were needed above. It was an accident. Unexpected things happen, Oliver. No one is to blame. How are we to enjoy life if we constantly worry about misfortunes besetting us? We all have good days and bad days, mishaps and blessings."

She was right, of course.

It wasn't humanly possible to control every circumstance, to completely protect those he loved. Yet more than ever he was compelled to admit the *Sea Gypsy* wasn't the place for her, as much as he wished it otherwise. He acknowledged full-on the risks a life at sea portended, and he'd not expose her to that peril.

Blaike belonged safely on shore, the lady of a grand estate, her every whim anticipated and met.

He gently separated the hair just to the right of her forehead. "The laceration isn't very big or deep, but you do have a sizable knot where you hit your head. Do you have a headache? I think we've powders somewhere. Maybe in the medicine chest."

Her shoulders quivered, and he firmed his embrace. She'd endured so much, been so brave and strong. A good cry might do her good.

The shaking grew stronger, and then she giggled.

Out loud and wholly delighted.

Oliver stiffened.

Blaike was laughing, not weeping?

M'Lady Lottie also giggled, sounding very much—alarmingly so—like Blaike, then proceeded to yell, "Time to shite" before flying back to her cage and doing just that.

Mortified, he shut his eyes.

That confounded cockatoo would be the death of him. How old had McMaster said those blasted birds live to? Thirty or more years?

What was Oliver to do with her for another decade?

Blaike laughed harder, fingers pressed to her middle in glee. "That bird is utterly awful."

Would she never cease to surprise him?

Where was the hysteria and self-pity most women would've displayed? The accusations and blame? The affront at Lottie's vulgar vocabulary? Instead, Blaike laughed, her beautiful bruised face glowing with humor.

"I'm sorry. But I'm imagining our homecoming. Both of us with lumps on our heads, my face." She swept her hand in the air. "Your shoulder." Her mirth subsided, and with a silly smile yet bending her mouth, she said, "We're quite the pair, aren't we? And lud. If you dare bring M'Lady Lottie ashore . . ."

Finding Blaike's humor contagious, he chuckled

before carefully kissing the bridge of her upturned nose.

Another fit of giggles overcame her. "I can only imagine the reactions. The censuring looks and slack jaws. The whispers and swishing fans. The theatric swooning."

He well could too, and that was why the cockatoo would never be introduced to Polite Society. Any society.

"I'd quite like to witness that, truth to tell." She wiped the tears of laughter from the corner of her eyes.

"I agree, we are quite a pair." How complete his life would be if only they could be life-long mates, too. With concerted effort, he forced his mind to another less melancholy topic. "You'll be happy to know, that other than a few bruises and abrasions, no one suffered any major injuries."

"I'm so glad. I fretted, wondering how everyone had fared. However, I knew I'd be a distraction and possibly put you or the others in danger if I disregarded your orders and went above deck." She slid a glance at Lottie preening her underwing. "That's why I came to see Lottie often. She helped occupy the time and my vivid imagination didn't run away quite so frequently."

He leaned away, and cupping her delicate shoulders, sought her eyes. "How is your sister?"

Toying with his shirt front, Blaike sighed.

Chagrin assailed him when she touched his soiled clothing. A homeless vagabond reeked less, but Blaike's nostrils hadn't so much as quivered.

"My sister's glad the ship has stopped trying to dump her from her berth every two minutes. Nonetheless, she vows she's never setting foot on a vessel bigger than a row boat for the remainder of her life."

Blaike pushed her hair behind her ear, revealing the slim column of her swan-like neck.

"She discovered, much to her relief, that although ginger tea didn't help with her *mal de mer*, hardtack did. I gave her mine as well since the biscuit worked such wonders. She's still asleep. Has been for hours now. Once the ship settled into a regular rhythm again, she was out like a snuffed candle."

A noise in the passageway reminded him they'd soon be interrupted. "I expect my bath or else a man to take M'Lady up top at any moment."

"Of course. I'll leave you then." She stepped away, her long hair swishing slightly with her movements.

At once Oliver longed to gather her back into his arms, but a whiff of stale sweat assailed him. Best wait until he'd donned fresh clothing.

"I ordered baths for you and your sister, too. Why don't you use my water since she's asleep, and I can bathe above?"

"You don't have to do that, Oliver. I'll wait." She touched his bearded jaw. "You're exhausted. I know you haven't slept. I'll come back in a few hours. We'll dine together, and you can teach me more about astronomy."

She leaned into him and whispered naughtily, "Or anatomy."

Cheeky, adorable wench.

"Wanton wagtail." Lottie flapped her wings, then sidestepped along her perch, head cocked.

"Lottie," Blaike scolded over her shoulder. "Say something nice."

"Luv-ly Lottie," the cockatoo promptly responded.

Oliver clasped Blaike's hand to his face, then turned the palm upward and kissed the tender flesh there.

"Il mio cuore è solo tua."

Fully above the horizon now, the sun's radiance burst into the chamber, and through the shimmering glass, a rainbow shone in the distance. The light and the colorful arc seemed somehow symbolic.

A sign.

Even after that horrendous storm, when he feared all might be lost, the blazing orb ascended to its usual place in the heavens.

Her expression at once playful and serious, Blaike clasped his hands in hers. "You did it again. Said something to me in Italian. It sounded very much like an endearment. Was it?"

Anticipation tinged her words.

Despite his best efforts not to encourage her affections, he'd failed. That such a woman cared for him humbled and exhilarated. Made him wish he had other options besides a lifetime at sea.

Tilting his head, not so very far because she was almost as tall as he, Oliver kissed her crown, pouring forth all the reverence he held for her in the swift, light touch of his lips.

"I said, *cara*, my heart is yours."

The gold flecks in her sapphire eyes glittered with unspoken emotion.

"And you love me."

A statement, not a question. Straightforward as always.

"Aye, I do."

Achingly, crushingly so.

Curse him for seven kinds of fool. The words he'd said in his head, in his heart, hundreds of times whispered forth. Three syllables that could change the course of his life forever.

"And you want to marry me."

God, was there ever a woman like her?

Hadn't he just vowed to do what was best for Blaike, to let her go?

"I do. More than I can express with mortal words."

The door rattled, announcing either his much anticipated bathwater, or the poor fellow who drew the short straw and was obligated to see M'Lady Lottie above deck.

Bestowing a beatific smile upon him, Blaike clasped her hands before her.

"Oliver. What are you waiting for? Ask me to marry you."

If only he could.

Even bruised and swollen, she was the most exquisite creature he'd ever seen.

"I . . ." How could he devastate her? This most precious treasure?

Brows drawn taut, she cocked her head and drew near him again.

"Is it because I haven't told you I love you, too?"

She laid her palm on his lapel.

"You must know I do, of course. So very, wonderfully much. And for such a long time." She gave a tinkling, self-conscious laugh, and dropped her gaze to the floor for a second. "I have, I think, since I first saw you striding across that ballroom looking very much like a dashing buccaneer. You rescued me that night, too."

Standing on her toes, she brushed her mouth against his, and electricity jolted to his bone's marrow.

It took every bit of self-control and dogged determination not to enfold her in his embrace, tie his chivalry and noble intentions to the ship's anchor, then toss them to the bottom of the Atlantic's depths for all time.

"My answer would be yes. As soon as feasible." Her eyes lit up impossibly more, her exuberant smile exposing her neat white teeth. "Can you marry us? I'm not sure if that's permitted, but wouldn't it be a marvelous surprise for my family?"

Loathing himself for what he was about to do— what he must do—even though carving his heart from his chest with a dagger would hurt less, Oliver grasped her upper arms. With all the tenderness he could husband, he set her from him.

"I'm not asking you to marry me, Blaike."

He firmed his hands briefly, conveying his earnestness.

"Not now. Not ever."

Shock mixed with utter anguish ravished her features.

"But why?" she managed, devastation now causing

the glistening in her eyes that a mere instant ago had held such joy. "I know you love me. I've seen the way you look at me, and you said so in your sleep. And I love you. Utterly and profoundly."

He'd said so in his sleep?

Bugger it. No wonder she'd been so buoyant. So confident.

Unable to look into her stricken gaze a moment longer, lest his noble intentions desert him, Oliver presented his back. For if he didn't, if Blaike vowed she loved him once more, his resolve would crumble like a termite infested log.

She touched his arm.

"Please. Oliver."

His whispered name forced past Blaike's tight lips, conveyed her life-altering torment and disbelief.

"Don't do this. Don't reject my love."

"Gentry and common bastards do not wed, Blaike. You live in a fantasy world if you think they do."

He did this for her sake. She'd understand someday. Eventually, when her emotions had calmed, reason would reign. And, in time, her heart would heal.

The pulverized organ that somehow managed to continue beating in his chest never would.

Hands fisted, spine rigid with suppressed emotion, he tucked his chin to his chest.

"Until we reach England tomorrow, Blaike, we should avoid each other."

Only an utter fool breathes the
slightest hint of a secret to a gossip. For
confidences like wild creatures, caught and
caged, escape the instant the door is opened.

~Scruples and Scandals
The Genteel Lady's Guide to Practical Living

15

Just over two weeks later, Blaike sat, ankles crossed, in the drawing room's window seat at Highfield Place House. Freddy, his soulful eyes observing her every move, rested his hoary snout on one of her thighs. An unopened book lay upon the other.

She fiddled with the edges of the novel's pages and puffed out her cheeks, releasing a long breath.

In recent days, she sighed far too often. It must be a symptom of the blue devils. How long did recovery from a mangled heart take?

No. The real question was how long before she stopped loving Oliver?

Pain lanced behind her breastbone once again, and she whispered lest anyone overhear and ask more prying questions, "I'll never stop. Ever."

Truth to tell, it sounded more like she made vow.

Freddy, ancient and decrepit now, perked his ears up and wiggled his bobbed tail as he licked her hand. Curled together on the navy brocade settee as they were wont to do, the equally aged cats, Pudding and Dumpling slumbered on.

Bending over, she rubbed Freddy's chest, his favorite petting spot.

"I missed you too, my sweet friend. I feared we might lose you before I returned home."

Life without the pudgy little dear would never be the same.

Wonder of wonders, she even missed M'Lady Lottie's raucous screeches.

Straightening, Blaike uncrossed her ankles and patted Freddy's thick back. "As soon as Blythe and Brette arrive, we'll go walkies. How's that? Even baby Leopold is permitted to go today, the weather is so mild. Doesn't that sound like fun?"

Not really.

Little stirred her interest lately, much less a walk in which she painted a false smile upon her face and pretended all was right with the bleak world.

Only in the past couple of days had the discoloration on her face faded to almost nothing, and she felt confident enough to venture out now. Although if she looked closely, there was the slightest greenish-yellow tinge on her cheekbone. A fine dusting of rice powder concealed the mark, else she'd not have agreed to the outing or having to explain yet again how she came by the injury.

After their walk today, the women had an appointment for the final fittings of their new gowns to be worn at this Friday's welcome home ball.

Blaike would've preferred to dispense with the folderol, including tonight's supper party, but the others wouldn't hear of it. Besides, her twin was so excited at the prospect of seeing everyone again, Blaike couldn't be the cross patch and ruin her fun.

Blaire's enthusiasm might have something to do with an expectation she'd see Lieutenant Drake. Blaike hadn't told her of his change in status after all. Not only did she not want to crush her twin, she didn't know exactly what his position was, and she refused to spread speculation. Blaire would know soon enough in any event.

Nothing remained secret for long in the *haut ton's* elite parlors or assemblies.

At least Blaike wouldn't have to worry about encountering Oliver and suffering that painful awkwardness. Once the family had learned of his role in rescuing the twins in *Port de Lyon* and again his masterful feat eluding the other vessel at sea, they lauded him a hero.

So far, and much to Blaike's relief—and consternation, bother it all—he hadn't accepted any of the many invitations sent his way and remained conspicuously absent

He'd not even seen her off the *Sea Gypsy*.

That had hurt awfully, his not bidding her farewell, and even gentle Blaire had commented on his lack of consideration.

A contrite, rather flustered, Mr. Hawkins had conveyed Captain Whitehouse's apologies.

Bitter tears stung, and she shut her eyes.

Simple everyday things—eating, speaking, *breathing*—took her full concentration. Her mind, the rebellious, undisciplined thing, continually turned to Oliver.

And the same question resounded over and over, the clamor never ceasing and even waking her each night after she'd finally fallen into a tormented sleep.

Why?

Even though she suspected he had acted out of a ridiculous honorable notion, she'd humbled herself and written him a letter asking him—pleading with him—to reconsider.

He hadn't replied.

A fresh wave of humiliation engulfed her. Nevertheless, she'd had to try.

Then, at dinner last week, Heath had mentioned Oliver intended to sail for the Caribbean soon, and implausibly, Blaike's heart fractured further. He truly meant to go on with his life, as if what had transpired between them had never occurred—meant nothing to him.

"There you are, dearest."

A sunny smile arcing her mouth, Blaire glided into the room, whilst tying her bonnet's lilac colored ribbons. The double ruffles of her elegant black embroidered lavender walking dress rustled with her movement. She'd regained a small amount of weight and healthy color once more brightened her cheeks.

Unlike Blaike, she glowed with happiness and couldn't disembark the *Sea Gypsy* swiftly enough.

Blaike's twin angled her head, disquiet crinkling the outer edges of her face.

"I'm worried about you, Blaike." After nudging Freddy aside, she sank onto the window seat's mulberry hued cushion. "I know you pine for Captain Whitehouse."

Blaike pulled her attention from the fashionably dressed passersby and searched her sister's compassionate countenance. No sense denying it. Her twin knew her too well. She lifted a shoulder.

"It will pass. These foolish things always do, don't they?"

It must. For a lifetime of this agony proved too awful to contemplate.

"*Hmm*, you cannot convince me of that," Blaire denied. "I may have been sick as death most of that horrendous crossing, but I do know you didn't return to our cabin until the early morning hours that first night. And I've seen how you look at the captain when you think no one is watching."

She squeezed Blaike's fingers. "He did the same, you know. Couldn't keep his gaze off you. I thought for certain . . ."

A sad, dismayed laugh escaped Blaike.

"As did I." She swept her hand across her forehead, almost as if she could wipe the memories from her mind. "He said he loved me. And in the next breath, he said he'd never ask me to marry him. 'Not now. Not ever.' His very words."

"Oh, Blaike, darling." Blaire rapidly blinked, her eyes shimmering with sympathy. "I'd like to plant him a facer for hurting you, the *roué*."

That was one French word Blaike understood well.

Emotion strangled her for a long moment, and she

almost crumbled under the pain rending her soul. "I just don't understand why he rebuffed me when I know he loves me, and he knows I love him."

"Nor do I." The lines of her mouth ribbon thin, Blaire too gazed out the beveled window, the diamond-paned leaded glass windows above showering them both in miniature rainbows.

Freddy settled more snuggly against Blaike, his tubby body shuddering with a contented groan. His light snoring and the clock *tick-tocking* atop the fireplace's Italian Bardiglio marble mantel filled the pregnant silence.

Laughter resounded in the hallway, and in a jiffy, the others bustled into the room, Brooke carrying her wee son. "Are we ready?"

She peered at Blaike and Blaire expectantly.

Blaike nodded. "Yes, I just have to put on my redingote and bonnet."

"Jenkin." Brooke addressed the butler. "Should his lordship return home early, please inform him we've gone for a stroll. Also, I forgot to mention, Mrs. Tremblay and her assistants are expected later for our fittings. Please show them to the floral salon when they arrive. Have Cook prepare light refreshments as well. Five fittings can be rather tedious."

In a trice, Blaike had donned her outer garments,

and the entourage, complete with Nurse pushing Leopold's pram, made for the park. The sunshine and the other foursome's excited chatter did help to ease Blaike's doldrums. The women had always been close, and she'd missed her sister and cousins terribly those awful months in Geneva.

That complete story had yet to be revealed, though Brooke and Heath had been apprised of Blaike's suspicions regarding Madame Beaulieu, as had Blythe and Leventhorpe.

At once, Heath had penned a letter to the ambassador.

Blaike couldn't bring herself to share the rest of the sordid tale quite yet.

Maybe she never would. What need was there?

Blaire would go to her grave with the knowledge.

If Blaike had actually been despoiled, and not just set upon, the risk of a child might've necessitated the telling. But by the grace of God, she'd been spared that degradation.

The sun warming their backs, Brooke and Brette strode arm in arm, each holding a parasol. Brooke held Freddy's lead as well, whilst Blaike and Blaire flanked a very pregnant Blythe. They too, carried unopened parasols. Across the way, the flush of pink and white cherry tree blossoms were visible near Kensington

Park's entrance.

Red squirrels darted across the plush lawns, pausing on their haunches every little bit, their tiny black noses twitching as they searched for predators.

As Blaike and the others strolled along, several of *le beau monde's* denizens warmly welcomed the twins home, while others, curiosity burning in their probing gazes, remarked on the premature return.

Blaike's and her twin's rehearsed response remained the same.

They'd missed their family far more than anticipated and with the birth of their new cousin, had opted to return home earlier than planned.

Those who looked upon them kindly accepted the explanation, and society's strictures silenced those inclined to prying.

Brooke glanced behind her, her cheeks glowing from the fresh air.

"I forgot to mention. Our numbers for supper tonight are slightly increased. Heath ran into an old friend of his at White's yesterday. Viscount Sethwick and his wife will join us along with Captain Whitehouse. The Viscountess owns quite an extensive shipping enterprise, and Heath wants to introduce her to the captain. He thinks it will be mutually beneficial." She turned her mouth up into a tolerant smile. "I did scold him for bringing a business element into our celebration of your return, but as Captain Whitehouse is a particular friend and we owe him such a debt of gratitude, I knew you wouldn't mind too terribly much."

Mind?

Was Brooke out of hers?

Of course Blaike minded.

She nearly gargled her tongue to mask her shock. Then the dread blanketing her.

Oliver at dinner.

No. no.

She just couldn't.

Not yet.

Not sit at the table with him and blather nonsensical twaddle, as if he hadn't torn her heart from her chest and tossed it upon the wharf for gulls to feast upon.

Blaire leaned forward, catching Blaike's attention. The question in her wide eyes fairly shouted, *What are you going to do?*

Fingertips pressed to her forehead, Blaike muttered to herself, rather more peevishly than she'd intended, "I do believe a megrim to rival Jupiter's has come upon me." Never mind that she'd never had a megrim in her life until this very moment. "I shall be forced to take to my bed at once, likely for days."

At least a week, until the *Sea Gypsy* weighed

anchor for warmer shores, carrying Blaike's love and heart with the vessel.

Blythe gave her a gimlet eye, then bent near and whispered for her ears alone.

"I hope you're not expecting one of us to clobber you with a hammer to alleviate your headache, as Jupiter requested. If I recall my Roman mythology correctly, it killed him. Besides, dear one, your head isn't what's aching. Your heart is."

Blaike shot her an astounded look. Was she so transparent?

Who else knew?

Brooke? Brette?

Likely, they all did.

Her focus shifted to their backs.

Was dinner someone's misplaced attempt at matchmaking?

She leveled a severe glance at Brette, notorious for her meddling in that department.

No, Heath couldn't know what had transpired between Blaike and Oliver. A coincidence was what this was, and she grudgingly admitted a beneficial one for Oliver. She'd mentioned Lady Sethwick to him herself.

Well, not by name, but by reputation.

She couldn't begrudge him the opportunity. But by Jove, she could be absent from dinner. She had all afternoon to contrive a believable excuse.

A sprained ankle was not out of the question.

Leopold cooed and giggled, and at once his doting aunties surrounded his pram, admiring the handsome babe with his mother's vibrant, almost violet eyes. The future Lord Leventhorpe would be a favorite of the ladies, to be sure.

"Best be careful, Brooke. We may spoil him." Brette chuckled as Leopold waved his little fists. Her regard sank to Blythe's swollen belly, and she half-winked. "That goes for your little one, too."

"You're a fine one to talk. In a few months, we'll have three darlings to simper over." Blaire motioned to Brette's less noticeable mound.

Brooke gave her son a doting smile and caressed his plump cheek. "A child can never have too much love, I don't think."

So caught up were they with the infant, they didn't pay attention to passersby. On such a lovely day, one expected crowded foot paths, to encounter acquaintances, perhaps extend an invitation to call or come for tea, or even witness a scandalous *tête-à-tête*.

Blaire's muffled gasp had four more pairs of eyes swooping to where she stared. She quickly schooled her dismayed features and turned her attention elsewhere, but not before Blaike saw the confusion in her eyes.

Lieutenant Drake strolled away from them on a

pathway across the greens, an elderly dame attired in black from her bonnet to her parasol on one arm and an attractive brunette in a superb jonquil walking gown on his other.

The woman Oliver had mentioned? And in public together, too.

Blast, now Blaike might—no would—have to explain to her twin.

Biting her lower lip, Blaire observed the lieutenant's progress from the corner of her eye.

He glanced their direction briefly, then saying something to his older companion, guided her down another pathway.

Had he glimpsed them, and that was why he'd steered his companions in the other direction?

Even as she formed the thought, he angled his head just the merest bit, cutting the Culpeppers another sideways look. Actually, his focus was riveted on one particular pale-faced Culpepper.

"Well, isn't this a pleasant surprise?"

An insightful lady knows well that secrets,
much like surprises, though favored by some,
are abhorred by others. Neither is right nor wrong.
~*Scruples and Scandals*
The Genteel Lady's Guide to Practical Living

16

N o. Not this too.
He couldn't be here.

Jonathon Severs just couldn't.

Not on top of everything else.

Nausea and fear battled for supremacy within
Blaike's bell.

Blaire's dismayed gaze collided with hers

Mustering every jot of self-control she had, Blaike
turned a bland gaze to him. Dressed like a popinjay, his
coat a shade this side of fuchsia and trimmed in Pomona
green, he rather resembled a parrot, right down to his
hooked nose.

Dread trotted a spiky path down her spine.

His leering gaze widened in appreciation as he took
in Blaike's sister and cousins. "I don't believe you ever

mentioned there were five of you, Miss Culpepper. Quite exceptional, I must say."

To a woman they responded with expressions frostier than a January dawn in Geneva.

His sister, wearing a smug smile, clung to her brother's arm, her manner more possessive than sisterly.

"Hello Blaire. Blaike. What a coincidence. We just arrived in London three days ago. Our elder sister, Anne, is to wed Lord Desmond in a fortnight." She angled her chin in a superior fashion. "He's an earl, you know. I doubt you've met him. Lord Desmond only travels in the highest circles."

Blaike had never mentioned her peerage connections to the pretentious twit. Titles weren't important to her, but she longed to rattle them off just to see Jacqueline's flummoxed expression.

When Blaike didn't return the Severs's greeting, Brooke slid her a puzzled glance. Savvy and possessing a keen intellect, she'd swiftly deduce something was as off as cream left in the sun for a week.

Brooke angled her head, appearing every bit the regal peeress. "May I ask how you are acquainted that you address my cousins so informally?"

Blaike didn't wait for an answer.

Spine rigid, she looped her arm through Blaire's, and wordlessly, they pivoted and strode in the other direction.

Never before in her life had she cut someone. But so help her God, the urge to beat Severs and his snotty sister to a pulp with her parasol so overwhelmed Blaike, her rage frightened her. She hadn't thought herself capable of such fury or of wishing someone bodily harm.

"Oh, Blaike," Blaire whispered, nearly running to keep up with Blaike's brisk pace. "What are we to do? Why are they here? Did you notice Jacqueline's snide—?"

"Snarl?"

For wasn't that how rabid animals behaved before they attacked? Blaike curled her lip in contempt. "How could I miss it? You can bet our sweet Freddy the others did as well."

"I'm sure of it." Blaire exhaled loudly. "What a deuced conundrum."

So much for keeping the surreptitious matter in Geneva quiet.

Dragging in a shaky breath, Blaike pursed her lips.

"I'll have to tell all. Then hope to God Raven, or Leventhorpe—or both—can threaten that bounder to such an extent, Jonathon will be forced to leave London. He doesn't dare even hint what he attempted. But his sister . . ."

Blaike's stomach flipped over like the time she'd eaten tainted fish and had been violently ill.

"She'll twist the truth. The tattle she contrives could cause damage to our family's standing." She squeezed her parasol handle so tight, it was a wonder it didn't snap under the strain. "I'm sure Heath and Tristan will think of a plausible—"

"Excuse. Yes, yes, of course they will. They're all powerful lords with many influential friends." Blaire dared a swift half-glance over her shoulder. "Those social climbing mushrooms don't know what they're up against."

She lifted her head and slid a covert glance toward where they'd last seen the lieutenant.

He'd disappeared from view.

Sadness deepened the contours of Blaire's pale countenance, and Blaike clamped her jaw because her beloved twin also faced heartbreak.

"Girls. Wait for us," Brooke called, as she and the others scurried to catch up.

Hardly girls anymore.

Blaike slowed, then stopped before turning with a forced upward bend of her mouth.

Probably looked more like a grimace than a smile. Even after several weeks, she wasn't ready to reveal the ugliness to the rest of her family. Odd since she'd had no qualms telling Oliver about the incident.

Honestly, though the ordeal had been traumatic and she could scarcely stand to look upon Jonathon Servers, she fretted more about *le beau monde's* reaction and how it would affect the others. Women and their families had been ostracized for less, even if the scandal weren't of their making or was no fault of theirs. Yet clandestine assignations were not unusual for married women.

She couldn't help but be galled by the hypocrisy.

Despite her intent to ignore them, her attention gravitated to the Severs. Arm in arm, they strolled in the other direction, their heads close together and apparently in an earnest conversation.

Plotting no doubt, the fiends.

Well, she'd not cow or hide in disgrace. She was the victim, and far past time women began to stand up against such assaults on their person instead of retreating in shame.

Again the notion of learning some sort of self-defense poked its head up. The idea didn't seem as farfetched as it once might have.

Radiant in a white embroidered muslin gown and breathless from her hurried walk, Blythe pressed a palm to her distended belly. She glanced downward and chuckled. "Someone didn't like Mama rushing about. I swear this babe is playing leap frog in there."

Brette touched Blaike's arm and angled her parasol's tip at the retreating Severs. "Whatever was that all about? I've never known you to be so abrupt."

A nicely worded way of saying rude.

Nurse was almost upon them with Leopold, his cheerful gurgles earning him an affectionate smile from the middling-aged woman.

Freddy, tongue lolling and eyes mere slits as he enjoyed the sunshine, sat inside the pram as well. Too much for the old boy to toddle to and from Highfield.

"Indeed," agreed Brooke, her gaze shifting between Blaike and her twin. "Though I expect you have good reason for abandoning your manners."

"I think it best we save that conversation for home." Blaike met each of their concerned gazes in turn as her twin made a sympathetic sound of agreement. "It's an unsavory tale and one I don't relish the telling of."

"Very well." Countenance contemplative, Brooke touched her chin with two fingers. "I don't usually form an opinion upon first meeting someone, but for those two I'll make an exception. That Miss Severs had the audacity to demand to know who we were. Must be an American custom, for I believe, given their accents, that's where they hail from."

Two laughing boys in deep blue and gray striped skeleton suits ran by in pursuit of a yapping Cocker Spaniel, dragging his lead.

"Jolly, come back here," called the elder boy.

They careened too near the pram, and Freddy barked, a weak, near-sighted warning.

Behind the lads, and holding a slightly older girl's hand, what had to be their frenzied governess scurried after the scamps.

"Masters Jesse and Travess. Stop chasing that wretched beast this instant!" Offering an apologetic smile, she bustled past the women while complaining to her other charge. "Miss Brianna, I do not know why they must always be into mischief. Frogs in the parlor yesterday, and a snake in the larder the day before."

The peach-clad girl shook her head, causing her neat russet ringlets to bounce.

"Why? Because they're boys, Miss Snowdrop, and all boys are made of snips and snails and puppy dog tails. Remember the poem?"

"And when they're young men they're made of sighs, and leers and crocodile tears. Add lies to that, too," the disgruntled governess huffed.

Even Blaike had to smile at the child's matter-of-fact explanation.

Brooke, however was having none of it. She bent

low and kissed Leopold's pudgy cheek. "Not a bit of it, my love. Snails indeed. Boys can be sugar and spice too."

Yes, cinnamon and cloves in particular.

Blaike could almost smell Oliver's scent, feel his lips sinking onto hers and his tongue plundering her mouth.

A much more somber troupe climbed Highfield Place House's stoop a quarter hour later than had departed.

No sooner had they reached the top step than the door swung open to a rather frazzled Jenkin.

"My lady, his lordship, as well as Lords Leventhorpe and Wycombe just arrived with Captain Whitehouse. And a *bird*."

Such disdain riddled his voice and puckered his face, at another time Blaike might've been amused.

Instead, she sucked in a great gulp of air and balked at the entrance so suddenly, Brette and Blythe plowed into her.

Oliver here? With M'Lady Lottie?

How could she bear to see him and not make a complete cake of herself?

"Sluice yer gob," came a familiar screech. "Blast and damn."

"Good heavens." Blythe peered around, seeking the culprit. "Who or what is that?"

"M'Lady Lottie," Blaike and Blaire said in unison.

So confounded did the others appear, Blaike offered by way of an explanation, "She's a salmon-crested cockatoo that spent several years in a—*erm*—house of ill-repute."

"This ought to be most entertaining." Blythe chuckled, while looking about for the bird again.

What had possessed Oliver to bring Lottie to Highfield?

Blaike wasn't noddy enough to believe he'd toted the bird along for a visit.

Still in a dither, the typically unflappable Jenkin rattled on as he closed the door, moisture actually beading his forehead and upper lip.

A first, that.

"That *creature* has stationed itself in a hanging pot in the solarium." Radiating disapproval, he elevated his chin and cinched his mouth.

"Jenkin?" Blaike said. "Where might we find the gentlemen?"

She wasn't about to specify one particular swarthy-skinned sea captain.

"In a bedchamber, Miss. There's been a fire on the captain's ship. The physician has been sent for."

A scrupulous woman knows that
much like diseases wastes the body, secrets
oft' tarnish the soul as do the scandals they cause.
~Scruples and Scandals
The Genteel Lady's Guide to Practical Living

Once Oliver's coughing fit ceased, he shrugged off Ravensdale and Leventhorpe's helping hands and collapsed onto the bed.

"I cannot think Lady Ravensdale will be pleased to have this fine counterpane stained with soot and smelling of burnt timber, canvas, and the Thames."

"My lady won't consider it for an instant," Ravensdale claimed and gave a slight shudder. "Lest you forget, she operated a dairy farm for years. Trust me, my friend, when I tell you that stench is not something easily forgotten. And we are all grateful beyond words for what you did for the twins. We are indebted to you, Oliver. A ruined bedcover is naught."

Rather than answer, Oliver grunted, momentarily overcome with angst.

The Sea Gypsy.

What would his crew do now?

They were good men, decent men, and they needed employment. For certain, a few might find positions on other vessels, but what about Hawkins? He wasn't a young man anymore.

At least Longhurst had insured the *Sea Gypsy*. He'd not fuss overly much at the ship's loss.

Why should he?

He never wanted any part of her except for Oliver's payments, and now Longhurst could collect the insurance, too.

For a flash, devastation rendered Oliver mute and immobile.

Now what did his future entail?

Hire on as a hand once more?

How could he when he'd captained his own ship these past years?

All was truly lost to him. Every hope and dream. Every ambition and goal. Gone up in orange flames.

After facing that dismal prospect, he forced his thoughts elsewhere, dredging up a speck of gratitude for what had been avoided. No hands had died, except Fairnly. No cargo yet loaded. His almost-paid-for ship had been anchored away from the docks, thus preventing a catastrophe beyond measure.

Three things to be grateful for.

Focus on those for now.

Time to fret about the other later. When his head didn't ache like a Lochaber Axe had been laid to his nape.

"Where's M'Lady Lottie?"

Raising his head a couple of inches, he peered about the finely appointed chamber.

"I take it you mean that evil-tempered, winged demon with a spear for a beak?" Leventhorpe scratched the bridge of his nose, then examined the crimson-stained handkerchief wrapped around his hand, covering the bite he received whilst helping haul Oliver onto the dock. "I think Jenkin chased her into the solarium. I've never seen the man so flustered. He actually bolted after her, flapping his arms and yelling. She called him a pimp whiskin."

Raising a brow, Wycombe grinned. "Somehow, I don't think our staid Jenkin appreciated being compared to a pimp. Wherever did she learn such language?"

"In a bordello," Oliver replied. "And Lottie was protecting me, Leventhorpe. That's why she bit you."

Why did that embarrass him?

His lesser station and lighter pockets had never caused him chagrin with these men, but a crazed bird from a whorehouse attacking those same friends did?

Devil a bit, his ravaged throat felt as if he'd swallowed glass shards. He eyed Leventhorpe's hand. "You probably ought to have that looked at. I have no idea how serious a bird bite can be."

"Sound advice, I think. The physician is expected shortly, in any event." Ravensdale leaned a shoulder against the bedpost, his intense scrutiny belaying his casual mien. "As is my wife, according to Jenkin."

Which meant Blaike would be here soon as well.

Oliver had counted himself fortunate that when they'd arrived the women hadn't been at home. He fully intended to depart just as soon as he could stand without the room spinning like a toy boat caught in a maelstrom. He'd not wanted to come here at all and protested loudly and strenuously against doing so.

Despite his objections, like fussy old tabbies, Raven, Leventhorpe, and Wycombe had bustled him into a carriage and made straight for Highfield Place House. They hadn't heeded his complaints, probably wrongly assuming manly pride motivated his reluctance.

They were wrong.

He'd refused each invitation thus far to spare Blaike more sorrow.

Why Ravensdale had insisted on inviting him here when he'd have preferred to meet at Lady Sethwick's

London office he couldn't fathom. He still hadn't come to terms with dining here tonight. Not that he'd be able to now, dressed only in a stained and torn lawn shirt, equally abused trousers and barefoot, to boot.

He couldn't even care for M'Lady Lottie now, much less a wife. What would become of the peevish cockatoo?

In a matter of hours, he'd been reduced to nothing.

More confirmation he'd made the right decision regarding Blaike, though he'd lived in a haze since seeing her disembark the *Sea Gypsy*. Careful to remain in the shadows, concealing his presence amongst the wharf's many buildings, he'd not been able to resist one final glimpse of her.

Pivoting in a slow circle, she'd surveyed the docks, and his heart had ripped asunder.

Not a doubt she searched for him.

And he hadn't a qualm that she loved him either, which made letting her go all that much more unbearable.

In obvious disappointment, her pretty mouth had turned down and her shoulders drooped the merest bit.

Impotent frustration had overwhelmed him, and he'd slammed his fist into the building's rough siding. He flexed his hand, his nearly healed cut and bruised knuckles a potent reminder of the folly of loving her and taking his rage out on unyielding wood.

Daring to peek at his friends from slitted eyes, he tensed at the pity edging each of their faces. Likely they knew full well everything he owned, save the clothing on his back, his mother's jewels hastily stuffed into a coin bag and tied with the string still hanging from his neck, and the bird raising a ruckus below were all he had to his name now.

There yet remained the small hope that Lady Sethwick might actually consider the clipper drawings he'd had sent round, or perhaps even have need of a ship's captain. That might've been discussed tonight, too.

That opportunity had gone up in flames as surely as the *Sea Gypsy* had.

Despair, second only to losing his beloved Blaike encompassed Oliver, and for a moment moisture stung his eyes.

"Whitehouse?" A tinge of alarm leeched into Leventhorpe's voice, and he poked Oliver's shoulder.

"I'm not incapacitated, nor do I need a physician or anyone fussing over me." Unless it was his sweet Blaike. He'd gladly accept her ministrations. Except he'd broken her heart, and now she most likely loathed him.

Particularly since he hadn't answered her letter.

He'd started to.

More times than he could count as the wadded foolscap littering his quarters could attest before they burned to cinders today. Yet every missive turned into a moonstruck swain's pathetic and not the least bit lyrical proclamation of devotion and adoration.

Ravensdale snorted his disapproval. "Nonetheless, you'll permit Dr. Barclay to examine you."

"Bloody blueblood, giving orders as usual," Oliver rasped, his voice hoarse as much from shouting as inhaling smoke. And swallowing a barrel full of river water as Lottie ranted her outrage whilst clawing his back.

"I don't suppose I need to remind you, that blue blood also runs in your veins." No real censure weighted Ravensdale's words.

An elbow across his gritty eyes, Oliver swallowed against the stinging of his raw throat and the cramping in his lungs. His shoulder complained no small amount as well. "I just breathed a bit of smoky air. I'll be fine."

"Old chap, that was more than a bit of smoke. Your ship lit up like someone torched a fireworks factory." Leventhorpe's dry retort earned him a glare beneath Oliver's crooked elbow.

"Probably because someone placed explosives on her."

By someone Oliver meant Fairnly, the turncoat.

It seems after the *Black Dove* limped into port last week, Abraham had bribed the blackguard. Only, the reckless idiot had blown his hand off and practically disemboweled himself. As he lay dying, he'd confessed all to Oliver.

Hawkins and Grover also witnessed the admission before Oliver realized the futility of fighting the spreading flames and ordered them over the Sea Gypsy's side. Surely with their testimony Abraham would see a noose now, or at the very least, the inside of a prison cell for a long while.

Raven's short chuckle relieved a jot of the tension in the bedchamber. "Queerest thing I've ever seen. You swimming toward the wharf with that obscenity screaming bird bobbing on your back. Drew quite a crowd."

"Do shut up, Ravensdale." Oliver needn't be reminded of the hooting and guffawing onlookers.

"Thank God you're all right, Whitehouse. I confess, I initially feared the worst. Pure luck we were on our way to Stapleton Shipping and saw the fire." This from Wycombe, a former rector.

Oliver ought to introduce him to Hawkins. They'd get along famously.

Where was Hawkins anyway?

He'd made it to shore, hadn't he?

Sudden fear stabbed behind Oliver's ribs. "Did

anyone see my first mate, Jack Hawkins?"

To a man they shook their heads.

"No, I'm afraid not." Wycombe swept Oliver a compassionate gaze. "We rushed to help you while others assisted your crew. I'm sure he's fine, however."

Ravensdale scraped a hand through his hair. "I'll send a missive to the harbor master and make an inquiry, if that relieves your mind."

"I'd appreciate it." If something had happened to Hawkins . . .

"Oliver?"

Blaike swept into the room, her lovely face taut with worry, and her bonnet clutched in one hand. She barely spared the other men a glance.

"My lords." In her typical, no-regard-for-what-is-customary-fashion, she bustled to the bed. After tossing her hat near his feet, she laid a hand on his good shoulder and bent over him.

"There was a fire? Aboard your ship? Is Abraham responsible, that snake? Are you hurt? Was anyone injured?" She threw a frustrated glance to the doorway. "Where is the doctor?"

Before he could answer, Miss Culpepper and Ladies Ravensdale, Leventhorpe, and Wycombe glided into the chamber, each still wearing their bonnets.

Hound's teeth. From their expressions, you'd think he'd died or was horribly maimed.

"Heath, what can we do to help the captain?" Lady Ravensdale asked, her tone fraught with worry.

Not a captain any longer. That truth shredded Oliver's already ragged soul further.

"Jenkin," said her ladyship, "send a footman to fetch one of his lordship's nightshirts, please."

The butler was here, too? Yes, just inside the doorway there.

Why not sell tickets and invite the whole of London? Oliver could well use the proceeds to keep out of the poor house.

Lady Ravensdale removed her bonnet and gloves, then passed them to the butler. "Also request wash water, and I think perhaps tepid tea with honey to soothe Captain Whitehouse's throat. Oh, and please send a note to Mrs. Tremblay asking her to come an hour later."

Jenkin accepted the other ladies' bonnets and gloves as well. "At once, your ladyship. I believe I heard the front knocker. I'll have Dr. Barclay escorted up straightaway and a footman bring a nightshirt."

"You wear a nightshirt, Raven?" Wycombe chuckled, low and teasing. "Cannot for the life of me picture that."

"*Shh*, darling." Lady Wycombe scooted to her husband's side. "It's not nice to poke fun at Heath just because you don't wear one."

Unused to being the center of so many concerned

glances, so much pity, or such warm regard, Oliver rather wished he could climb beneath the bed. He closed his eyes lest any of his friends see the sudden moisture that blurred his vision.

"Blaike," Lady Leventhorpe said, "is the poor captain unconscious?"

"I am not, your ladyship." Stifling a groan, he sat up. "And I'm not injured either, so there's no need for fussing or nightshirts. I'll take my leave momentarily."

Where he'd go, shoeless and without a groat, he hadn't determined yet.

"The devil you will." Raven's grim countenance brooked no arguing. "I'll not hear any more of that gibberish. You'll reside here for the foreseeable future."

Oliver would see about that.

"Oliver, be careful." Blaike grabbed the pillows, and as she had aboard the *Sea Gypsy,* tucked them behind him. "There, now lean back." A smile ticked her mouth up on one side. "This is getting to be a habit, me taking care of you."

Aware of the multiple pairs of eyes trained on their every move, he swallowed, then cleared his throat.

Finally, more for something to distract them from his pathetic state, and their avid glances swinging between him and Blaike, he lifted the gems from around his neck. He took Blaike's hand and placed the pouch atop her palm.

"These were my mother's. I'd be honored if you'd accept them."

Too bold by far and assuredly beyond the mark.

Women didn't accept gifts from men unless they were from a family member or their betrothed. He could never sell the set though; even if it meant he'd face debtor's prison. And there was no one else he'd rather have the jewels. Besides, on London's streets, he'd likely be robbed of the emeralds in a trice. Far, far better Blaike have them than take the risk of his mother's most prized possession being hawked.

Attention riveted on the exchange between him and Blaike, no one made a sound.

Fair brow puckered, she loosened the cinched leather closure, and then dumped the contents on the bed.

From the bedside window, soft late morning sunlight illuminated the brilliant green and white stones.

"Her gems?" She picked up a comb and ran her pointer finger across the bright jewels. A shrewd look entered her startling blue eyes before she narrowed them, pinning him to the fluffy pillows. "You told me she meant these for your wife."

Blaike didn't think . . .?

No. No. She couldn't.

Not after what he'd said aboard the *Sea Gypsy*. He'd been perfectly clear. Brutally clear.

One of the women in the chamber made an odd sound.

He couldn't be sure which, since he'd lost the ability to drag his gaze from Blaike. As he tried to figure out what she was about, and how to gently unravel this new bumblebroth, a satisfied yet challenging smile curved her dewy mouth.

From below, voices echoed in the entry, and a bird's chirrup carried through the window pane.

"Not the most romantic proposal, to be sure." She slipped the ring on one finger, then another. "I fear it's a trifle big."

It dawned on him then.

She knew exactly what she was about, the minx.

He'd carelessly opened the door, and she'd snatched the opportunity like a starving urchin clutches a dropped half loaf.

"Blaike . . .?"

She wouldn't dare go that far. Wouldn't twist his words and his intentions. Wouldn't exploit his oversight and trap him.

Would that be so very awful?

"Then again, you don't generally do things the conventional way, do you, Oliver?" She shook her head, her pearl earrings swaying with the motion. "That's one of the things I most love about you. You do the unexpected."

She was one to talk.

"Truth there," Raven, or it might've been Leventhorpe, muttered, his voice so brimming with amusement, Oliver bit his tongue to keep from telling him to sod off.

This wasn't funny.

Actually, had it been someone else, he'd have been highly entertained as well.

He searched Blaike's guileless face. She'd admitted to loving him in front of everyone. No hint of bashfulness or uncertainty flushed her cheeks or shadowed her expressive eyes.

"I rather prefer being unorthodox myself. It's so freeing." She grasped his hand and held her other up, admiring the ring's oval setting.

The glance she lowered to Oliver held such love and adoration, it awed him.

Humbled him.

Frightened the hell out of him.

"I accept. How soon do you want to wed? As soon as the banns have been read?"

A woman of noble character knows
that secrets and lies go hand in hand, and
our greatest secrets are the lies we tell ourselves.
~Scruples and Scandals
The Genteel Lady's Guide to Practical Living

18

And there it was.

Everyone started jabbering at once, but the buzzing in Oliver's ears muffled their exact words. He thought he heard exclamations to the effect of, "Silliness, acting rashly, unbecoming behavior, isn't done, unscrupulous and scandalous."

Blaike remained stoic, her pert chin angled in defiance. "Thank you for your concern, but this is a conversation between Oliver and me. I assure you, it's not the first time we've discussed marriage."

It almost sounded conceivable, perhaps even respectable, the way she said it.

Disapproval pulling the planes of his face taut, Raven's reproachful gaze took in each of the other men in the room, one by one. "Why I should be surprised you didn't approach me first, Whitehouse, when neither Leventhorpe nor Wycombe bothered to either, I cannot fathom. Yet I am."

Blaike still held Oliver's hand, only now she clung to him, as if she needed his support and strength. Yes, she had acted imprudently and impulsively, and God help him for a smitten fool, he loved her all the more for her courage to seize what he'd been too afraid to pursue.

The bed squeaked slightly as he adjusted his position.

Never would he humiliate her by publically denouncing her impetuous, and perhaps, slightly foolhardy decision. Didn't he also know what it was to love so desperately?

"Where is he? In there?" demanded an imperious, but distinctly refined voice, followed by the rhythmic thumping of a walking stick banging upon a wooden panel in the corridor.

Blaike withdrew her hand from Oliver's, and also removed the ring and placed it with the other gems but didn't budge from her station beside his bed.

"I say, where *is* my son?"

Willoughby.

Bloody maggoty hell.

Could this day get any worse?

How had he learned of Oliver's mishap?

Hawkins, the interfering busybody.

Likely he feared Oliver had nowhere to go and no one to turn to, so he'd rounded up anyone and everyone the first mate thought might help.

That was where he'd disappeared to the moment he'd made the wharf. Good thing the *Sea Gypsy* likely lay at the bottom of the River Thames, for Jack Hawkins no longer held the first mate position.

"Father, if you'd permit the majordomo, he'd direct you."

Lionel Talbot, Oliver's half-brother also?

Oliver cut Blaike a sideways glance.

Jaw sagging, she gaped at the doorway before she tore her attention away. "Oliver? Is that your family?"

He gave a terse nod and clamped his teeth as a feminine voice joined the others.

"Yes, Papa. You mustn't be so impatient."

Which sister, Vivian or Sylvia?

"Sylvia is right. You'll only upset Oliver further, Papa. Isn't that so, Doctor?"

Of course the other sister was here, too.

The whole deuced family. Had they brought their spouses and broods of offspring?

"As I haven't examined the patient yet, I cannot make that determination. Mr. Drake, you might be in a better position to answer Miss Talbot's question since you claim a close friendship with the captain." More than a hint of annoyance weighted the good doctor's tone.

Oliver did groan then.

Drake too?

What in God's name had Hawkins told them?

That he lay dying?

Blaike sank to the mattress, concern pleating the corner of her eyes. "Are you in pain?"

Oliver spared her a haggard glance. "Aye, agony, but it's not physical."

"I presume that open door is my son's chamber?"

Arrogant sot, claiming his fatherly prerogative.

"Captain Whitehouse's chamber is just here. If you'd lower your walking stick and permit Dr. Barclay to pass? " Jenkin's request was dry as ash and just as acerbic.

When Oliver had Hawkins alone . . .

Six more people crowded into the already overly full bedchamber.

Make that seven.

The footman arrived with a folded nightshirt, which Oliver had no intention of donning whilst still breathing. However, unlike the other intruders, once the servant had delivered the garment, he beat a hasty retreat.

"Sir, a missive arrived for you a short while ago."

Jenkin passed Oliver the note.

Hawkins's familiar scrawl lashed the neatly folded paper. Best read it later when Oliver's curses wouldn't offend the ladies. He handed it to Blaike. "Would you put that on the bedside table for me, please?"

"Of course."

Oliver exchanged nods with his sire, brother, and Drake who immediately sought Blaire, but only offered her the merest cant of his head in greeting.

Rather than respond in kind, she remained bland-faced and turned her regard back to Oliver.

Blaike must've told her twin about Drake's change in circumstances.

Oliver's sisters each swooped in to kiss his cheek, as if he were a most treasured brother.

"I'm so relieved you aren't seriously hurt." Sylvia gave him a watery smile, and the most peculiar sensation rattled around the vicinity of his ribs.

"Drake, might I ask why you are here?" Oliver had guessed the truth of it, but wanted confirmation.

"Hawkins sent word. It sounded serious." Drake didn't seem the least apologetic for intruding. He pulled a crumpled scrap from his pocket. "Actually, the note was brief. *Explosion SG. All lost in fire. Captain gravely injured. At Ravensdale's*."

First time Oliver had ever known Hawkins to

stretch the truth.

"Is it true then, Oliver?" Worry lined Sylvia's pale face as her gaze skittered over him, from head to holey-stockinged toes. "You're hurt?"

"I was injured in *Port de Lyon*. Shot, if you must know." Oliver wasn't about to tell them Blaike had cared for him.

He swept his family a cool glance. Why couldn't he accept their warm regard? Why must he always keep them at arm's length?

Mamma. That was why.

"Hawkins notified all of you as well?" Oliver asked.

"No, just Father." Vivian's attention gravitated to Blaike sitting beside Oliver for the third time. "Did you forget? Our families have tea together on Mondays."

How cozy.

Her cheeks pinkened, and she shot Oliver an abashed look. "You've been invited numerous times too, Oliver."

He had. And never responded to a single invitation.

Wasn't he the churlish sod?

After greetings had been exchanged, Dr. Barclay took charge. "I need to examine my patient, if you please."

He looked pointedly at the door.

"Doctor, Lord Leventhorpe should have his hand examined as well." Blaike had noticed, Leventhorpe's injury, had she?

Dr. Barclay glanced to where she pointed. As he puttered in his bag he asked, "What happened, my lord?"

Leventhorpe glowered at his makeshift bandage. "A cranky cockatoo wanted a taste of me."

That elevated Dr. Barclay's grizzled brows several inches. "A cockatoo, you say? Don't believe I've ever treated a bird's bite before. I'll tend you when I've finished with Captain Whitehouse."

"Why don't we all go through to the drawing room, and I'll have a light repast prepared?" Lady Ravensdale held her arm out, indicating the others should go before her.

Everyone but Blaike, her twin, and Willoughby filed out.

"Blaike? Aren't you coming?" Her sister, one hand resting on the door jamb, paused at the entrance.

Blaike reluctantly stood, then brushed Oliver's hair off his forehead. "Yes. I'll come back when the doctor says I might." She faced Willoughby and dipped into a half curtsy. "I look forward to conversing with you below, my lord."

Willoughby inclined his gray streaked head. "And

I you."

"We'll speak later, Captain," she said, skirting the bed.

Back to propriety was she?

Because of Willoughby's presence?

With an unreadable final glance at Oliver, she accepted her twin's arm, and they departed.

"That young woman is in love with you." Willoughby, still hovering at the foot of the bed, leaned on his elaborate walking stick.

"I know, but—"

Before Oliver could finish, Willoughby's attention sank to the gems scattered beside Oliver's thigh, and he inhaled a ragged breath. He came round the side of the bed. His haughty countenance softening, he lifted the necklace.

"I gave these to your mother the first time I proposed."

Though there are no bars or
locked doors, a long kept secret can still
imprison one. Consider carefully the cost of freedom.
~Scruples and Scandals
The Genteel Lady's Guide to Practical Living

19

Oliver didn't seem perturbed.

Half listening to what Mr. Maddox sitting to her left said, Blaike observed Oliver from beneath her lashes.

My, but he looked so different.

Wearing borrowed evening clothing, his beautiful midnight hair shorn and beard shaved, he appeared every bit the proper English gentleman. Relaxed and amiable, a ready smile upon his firm mouth, his infamous glower hadn't put in an appearance the entire evening.

Earlier, when he'd entered the drawing room with his new fashionably short hair and clean-shaven face, the others' compliments had muffled her stifled gasp. She'd thought him striking before, had adored his long hair and beard, but now?

Well, he quite took her breath away.

In the most feminine, fluttery manner.

Blaike glanced across the table for the umpteenth time.

His tanned cheeks contrasted with his well-defined, slightly paler jaw.

Ninny, stop staring.

Her gullible heart pattered faster, as it had whenever her eyes met his tonight.

Thank goodness, Dr. Barclay had declared him none-the-worse from escaping the fire aboard the *Sea Gypsy,* but had prescribed an abundance of fresh air to cleanse Oliver's lungs. Such a thing wasn't to be had in London, for Town's skies were notoriously sooty.

Much to her astonishment, the good doctor had praised Blaike's care of Oliver's shoulder. Nonetheless, he expressed the merest concern that infection might set in after the dip in the less than pristine Thames. Promising to return in a couple of days, the doctor left instructions about what signs to look for, and he was to be sent for at once should any symptoms occur.

Dropping her focus to the roast partridge on her plate, Blaike wadded her napkin as remembered panic stalled her breath for a moment. Such terror had gripped her when Jenkin had said there was a fire. Even now with Oliver sitting but feet away from her, hale and hearty, her stomach remained woozy. How he'd managed that swim with his shoulder not completely healed, she couldn't comprehend.

Sensing his perusal once more, she lifted her head.

He sent her a dazzling smile, so intense, she quivered from neck to knee. From the confident arcing of his black brow, he knew how he affected her.

This genial demeanor was good, wasn't it?

There'd been no opportunity for them to talk, but surely he wouldn't be this affable if he remained vexed with her. Truth to tell, for a man who'd just lost his ship, he didn't appear wholly devastated.

Quite the opposite, in fact.

She couldn't put her finger on exactly what, but there was something different in his comportment aside from the drastic change in his appearance. Whatever had transpired between Oliver and his father had transformed them both.

While they'd waited for Dr. Barclay to finish examining Oliver, no one had mentioned that awkwardness of Blaike's peculiar potential betrothal. How could they, with guests present?

That was the one unfortunate rub in all of this.

Mr. Drake—strange to not call him lieutenant any longer—had been most reserved in his attentions to

Blaire. Truthfully, other than the cursory hello, he'd not spoken to her, yet his gaze continually followed her 'round the room.

To her twin's credit, Blaire acted the composed woman of refinement, chatting and smiling with their visitors, and not once did she turn soulful eyes to him.

Blaike knew full well the supreme effort that façade had cost her sister.

She hadn't completely escaped repercussions for her wild impulse in Oliver's chamber, however. After the guests had departed, and as the women excused themselves to go to their fittings, Heath had taken her aside. He'd asked to see Blaike in his study tomorrow morning. At ten o'clock sharp. Likely to chastise her unseemly, impetuous, and shameful behavior.

A smile pulled her mouth upward.

Dear Heath. He'd had no idea what he'd taken on when he married Brooke and was appointed the other four Culpeppers' guardian. He'd done remarkably well for a man with no sisters.

She supposed it would be the perfect time to tell him about the Severs, too.

Along the length of the table, the guests laughed and chatted, their conversations mixing with clinking china and silverware. And every now and again, a raucous, muffled call filtered into the dining room from a disgruntled M'Lady Lottie, sequestered in the solarium.

Somehow, someone had managed to procure a good-sized cage, and Blaike had helped gather items for the bird to play with as well as food for the cockatoo.

She'd spent several minutes soothing the frazzled creature, and couldn't contain her jubilant smile when Lottie obediently toddled onto her perch repeating, "Purdy bird, purdy bird. Purdy, purdy, birdy, bird."

A mortified gasp replaced her upturned lips when, a moment later, M'Lady Lottie turned to Heath, fanned her salmon crest, and said in a woman's coy voice, "Shag fer a shillin', guv."

His eyebrows had vaulted toward his thick hairline before he replied through his laughter, "Alas, my wife won't permit it. But thank you for the kind offer."

"Raven. For shame." He'd received a sharp rap on his arm from Brooke for his tasteless humor.

Oliver turned to address something Lady Sethwick said.

That appeared to be going splendidly, and Blaike had the absurd childish desire to clap her hands in delight at his good fortune. For certain, he deserved some grace. Fate hadn't been altogether kind to him.

He nodded at whatever her ladyship said, and a shock of hair fell over his forehead, just above his scar.

Canting her head, Blaike considered him.

No denying his cropped hair became him. Why had he decided to have the rest lopped off, and his beard too?

A small stab of alarm had her squeezing the wine goblet's stem.

Had that to do with his father, too?

Was it possible, Oliver had fashioned a plan about his future so swiftly?

Did it include her?

She took a sip of wine, as another hot flush engulfed her at her gumption in his chamber. Of course she'd known he wasn't proposing, and she was fully aware she'd backed him into a corner, so to speak. Naturally, she had no intention of forcing herself on him. But if misplaced honor and pride were what prevented him from asking for her hand, then she'd fight for Oliver.

Fight for their love.

Make him fight for it, too. If that was what he wanted as much as she did.

Didn't he realize not everyone was fortunate enough to find the one who made their heart and soul whole?

Nothing to do if Oliver truly wouldn't marry her.

She'd not humiliate herself any further.

In fact, Blaike very well might accept the Sethwicks' generous offer to visit Craiglocky Castle.

Anytime, they'd said. She'd never been inside a medieval keep before, let alone stayed in one. It might prove just the distraction she needed.

If Oliver couldn't be persuaded to see reason.

To let love guide him and trust what came after.

Dinner dragged on for hours, it seemed, as did the men's brandy and the ladies' tea afterward. At long last, everyone gathered in the drawing room.

Blythe made straight for the mahogany pianoforte and Lady Sethwick joined her. In a moment, their expert playing filled the room.

Near the fireplace, Oliver chatted with Lord Sethwick and Heath. He ran a finger over the marble mantel and said something to Heath. After Heath responded, Oliver smiled and gave a brief bow, then headed in Blaike's direction.

The moment was at hand. He meant to discuss her impulsive act, sure as feathers stuck to warm tar.

Her palms dampened, and she swallowed.

He didn't appear the least bit angry, but she was still nervous as a goose the week before Christmastide.

Her future might be decided within the next few minutes.

Well, her future with Oliver. At least she'd know, one way or the other.

She stubbornly disregarded the maddening little

voice that reminded her he'd already had his say aboard the *Sea Gypsy*.

He bowed before her chair, his gaze holding a silent message. Good or bad, she couldn't discern. Neither could she decide if she preferred this refined man or the unpolished captain who'd first stolen her heart.

"Ravensdale has said I might take a turn about the solarium with you since it's begun to rain, and I cannot take the stroll I'd anticipated."

My, he sounded every bit the polished gentlemen. Where had her swaggering buccaneer gone? He'd anticipated a stroll with her, had he?

Blaike rose, acutely aware every eye in the room had turned to them. More than one pair of lips turned upward knowingly. She'd got herself into this conundrum, and she'd have to deal with the consequences.

"I'm sure M'Lady Lottie will be happy to see you. She said pretty bird today."

"Yes, and a great number of other less polite things as well," Leventhorpe offered dryly as he stood beside his wife, turning the music pages.

"Shall we?" Oliver extended his elbow.

The solarium lay along the corridor on the opposite side of the house. More nervous than she could ever recall being with him, Blaike searched for something to break the strained silence.

"Why did you cut your hair and shave your beard?"

Oliver ran a hand over his smooth jaw, and offered a lopsided smile. "I thought I might make a better impression on Lady Sethwick if I didn't look like an ill-kempt marauder."

"No such thing," Blaike denied. "Your long hair was lovely."

They'd reached the solarium, and he opened the door.

Candles burned in several sconces on the walls, and the sweet perfume of Brooke's prized gardenias tinged the humid air. Lottie's new cage had been placed beneath a pair of potted ficuses, and some large leafed plants formed a half circle behind the cage.

"Hello, Lottie."

Immediately upon spying Oliver, she launched into her usual dancing and bobbing as Blaike covertly twisted the key in the keyhole.

"Ol-eeve. Ol-leeve."

"I don't think she's ever going to pronounce your name correctly."

Blaike unlatched Lottie's cage, and at once the cockatoo soared through the airy room, weaving and dipping before landing on a hanging pot. Truth to tell, the greenhouse would make an ideal over-sized birdcage for her and even slightly resembled her native habitat.

Oliver remained silent, his ebony gaze never leaving Blaike.

Uncomfortable under his intense scrutiny and uncertain why he hadn't yet broached the subject that was at the forefront of both their minds, she made her way to the wicker sofa with it's coral, yellow, and sage floral cushion. After tossing a matching pillow aside and settling on the seat, she plucked a couple of dead blossoms from the salmon colored begonia atop the matching wicker table.

The silence dragged on, until her nerves became taut and her stomach wobbly, and she feared her dinner might reappear. Oh, how she dreaded hearing what Oliver in his pity or compassion couldn't bring himself to say.

Fine then.

She'd spare them both the prolonged discomfit.

Better to have it done and over.

"Oliver, I apologize for placing you in such an uncomfortable position earlier. That was unfair of me and manipulative as well. You made yourself absolutely clear that day in your quarters. I . . . ." How could she tell him that she'd hoped—prayed—he'd changed his mind? Wanted to beg him to give their love a chance.

I shan't cry.

Head slanted, she focused on Lottie preening her feathers rather than his beloved features. Her heart would shatter, loudly and in as many pieces as dropped crystal, if she had to witness the relief in his expression when she told him what she must.

Closing her eyes briefly, she inhaled a fortifying breath. She wasn't a whiny, weak-kneed miss. She'd take responsibility.

"Of course I shan't hold you to that ridiculousness. Neither will I ask you to be the one to tell my family. After all, you heard their reactions in your chamber. They won't be the least surprised."

Why didn't he say something?

Gritting her jaw against the pulsing ache in her throat, she commanded the moisture in her eyes to go.

I. Shall. Not. Cry.

He'd wandered to one of the gardenia bushes, and now held one of the fragile blooms in his sun-browned hand. "You've changed your mind then?"

A lady of discernment bears in
mind that just because someone reveals a
secret, it doesn't mean they're telling the truth.
~Scruples and Scandals
The Genteel Lady's Guide to Practical Living

20

"**N**o. I assumed . . ."

Blaike wet her lower lip, and brows scrunched, peered at him. Finally, she managed, "I don't know what to say to make things right, Oliver."

A traitorous tear fell onto her hands folded in her lap.

The drops would ruin the fine satin.

This pale cerulean and ivory gown, with its delicate blue roses embroidered at the hem, cuffs and neckline had been selected because it made her eyes appear bluer and her skin creamier. She'd chosen it to impress him. Had wanted to be pretty for him.

"I love you. I tried to stop, because I know you said you would never ask me to marry you. But, God help me, I swear I cannot."

Head tucked to her chest, she whispered the last words, and in that moment knew them to be true. She would never, could never, cease loving Oliver. Some women were meant to love a single man. It seemed she was one of them.

"*Amore mia*, I don't want you to."

Then Oliver was beside her, gathering her into that wonderfully strong embrace she yearned for and remembered so well.

His unique manly essence combined with soap, and the brandy he'd imbibed after dinner drifted to her nostrils. Eyes closed, she breathed him in, this man who'd become such a vital part of her life. She'd do anything for them to be together. Even toss her scruples aside and risk scandal, so great was her love.

Oliver spoke into her hair. "I've regretted those words every second since I stupidly, cruelly uttered them. Please tell me you can forgive me."

"Of course I forgive you." Blaike smiled and touched his cheek. "I forgave you as soon as you said them. When you love someone, forgiveness comes easily."

A door slammed shut somewhere in the house, and laughter carried down the corridor. Either Lady Sethwick or Blythe continued playing the pianoforte.

He grasped her hand and brought it to his lips,

giving each knuckle a reverent kiss.

"Tonight, *cara,* I finally saw reason. With humility and the full knowledge of how very blessed I am to have your love, I implore you to marry me."

At once her vision blurred, and she struggled to speak. "Truly, Oliver?"

"Aye, truly, *bella, Ti adoro.*"

"What made you change your mind?" Threading her hand through his hair, enjoying the thick, silky strands sliding between her fingers, she said, "I'm positive it wasn't my rash behavior in your chamber. No one makes Captain Oliver Whitehouse do something he doesn't want to."

Holding her tighter, he laughed, a warm self-deprecating sound.

"Actually, my father revealed long held secrets to me, and now I understand so much." He kissed her damp cheeks, then her mouth for a splendid, far too short moment. "He'd asked my mother to marry him, several times truth to tell, but she refused."

Blaike stiffened and angled to stare into his tender gaze, not at all sure she'd heard him correctly. "Why would she do that? You told me she adored him."

A violent gust of wind pelted rain against the glass.

Startled, Lottie flapped her wings. "Hooligans. Bolt the door."

Secure within Oliver's embrace, Blaike snuggled closer. Let the storm vent her wrath. Nothing could disturb her contentment.

"She did love my father. But *Mamma* felt unworthy, and claimed commoners and aristocrats shouldn't marry."

That sounded far too familiar.

Oliver had said that exact thing.

"According to my father, *Mamma* vowed those unions caused untold difficulties and heartache. She believed if they married, it would bring shame upon Father's dynasty, and she feared it would eventually taint their love."

Did he realize he'd been referring to Willoughby as his father since this morning?

Brushing his smooth jaw with her fingertips, Blaike shook her head, confused.

"Balderdash. She must've endured shame and ridicule bearing a child out of wedlock. Look how it affected you? Didn't she consider that?"

Oliver leaned back, drawing her with him until she practically lay beneath him. "She did, and yet she still wouldn't marry my father or even let him set her up in a house. You see . . ."

He paused to kiss her collarbone, then trailed his tongue across the quivering flesh to her shoulder.

Such bliss infused Blaike, it was all she could do to keep her thoughts straight and not forget all and ravish him.

"Go on," she managed, hardly recognizing her own passion-laden voice.

"I'd much rather kiss you, and give you that anatomy lesson you requested." Oliver's husky tone suggested he was as overcome as she. "Except I fear we might be interrupted. That might prove a mite awkward."

"We won't be disturbed." She waggled her brows, a naughty smile tugging her mouth sideways. "I locked the door."

"Why you sly wench you." He tickled her ribs, and she giggled.

Who was this playful devil?

"You can give me a lengthy lesson afterward. In fact, I insist upon it." Perhaps—hopefully—a whole lot more than kissing might occur. Well, not too much more. For certain, someone would be along soon to ensure propriety wasn't breached.

She nudged Oliver in the ribs. "What is this secret the viscount told you?"

"Father confessed he didn't know everything either. Only what *Mamma* had shared after the last time she refused his suit. It seems my grandmother—my *nonna*—was the youngest and favorite daughter of an Italian nobleman, Francesco Rossini. She fell in love with *Nonno*, a humble shipbuilder, and eloped when my great-grandfather forbade them to see each other. Her father disowned her—never spoke to her again."

"How cruel. It must've broken her heart."

Blaike shifted, and the wicker creaked. Surrounded by windows on three sides, the solarium still held the day's heat, despite the cranky weather outside.

"I think it did. But my great-grandmother wrote letter after letter, trying to persuade *Nonna* to return home. Without her husband. Or her child of sin. *Nonna* was Catholic, but *Nonno* wasn't, and so her mother condemned their child too."

"I don't believe I like your great-grandmother at all."

"Nor I. According to my father, my great-grandmother blamed my *nonna* for everything from her father's ill-health and losing his sight, to her married sister running off with her lover, and her brother's sons drowning and leaving no male heirs."

"That's awful. She sounds like a spiteful, bitter woman." What kind of a person did that to their child?

"She only stopped when *Nonna* died. By her own hand. My *mamma* found her. That's when *Nonno* moved to England and changed his name from de

Casabianca to Whitehouse so the Rossinis couldn't find them. After a few years they did though. Another sister wrote *Mamma* once in a while, usually to announce a death or a marriage in the family."

"Oliver, do you think those are the letters?" Blaike's eyes rounded in distress. "Oh, no. Did they burn, too? Now you'll never know—"

He placed two fingers on her lips. "*Shh*, don't fret, *cara*. I took your advice and had the entire packet, the letters and the documents, translated."

Exhaling a great puff of air, she relaxed once more. "I'm so relieved. And I confess, terribly curious."

"I wish *Mamma* hadn't been so afraid. Today, after Father told me what she'd done, I realized I was following in her footsteps. Forsaking the one I adore for fear of society's strictures and what might happen."

Blaike sighed, and draped an arm about Oliver's brawny shoulders. "It's not for us to judge your mother for her decisions. Unless someone has been in the same circumstances, experienced the same trauma, they haven't any right to say what should or should not be done. Even then, they shouldn't."

"Now you sound like Hawkins." Oliver shook his head, his lips quirked in exasperation. "You know that note he sent?"

She nodded. "Yes."

"He apologized for overstepping the bounds, but said I was too pig-headed to accept help from those who care about me. So he'd taken matters into his own hands. He also said he'd call on me when he returned from visiting his daughter in Deal." A rueful smile tipped Oliver's mouth. "I didn't even know he had a daughter."

"What will he do for work now?"

"Lady Sethwick assures me she can find him a position, but I've half a mind to make him our butler. If you're in agreement."

One of Blaike's winged brows twitched. "Our butler? We don't have a house."

More on point, what would Oliver do now?

He pushed her gown off one shoulder, and as he nibbled his way to her neck, slid one hand up her thigh. "*Ti desidero*."

Good heavens.

Forget the reading of the banns.

That took much, much too long.

She'd demand they be wed by special license.

He caressed a particularly sensitive spot on her hip, and she all but dissolved into a mass of desire.

Tomorrow.

Yes. They must be wed tomorrow.

He edged her bodice lower.

"Pretty bubbies," M'Lady Lottie cried.

Blaike and Oliver both burst out laughing, and he left off his explorations.

"When we are married, she'll not be anywhere near our bedchamber. In fact, I'm searching for a mate for her. Maybe that will keep her occupied." He sat up, then smoothed his hair. "We should get back and announce our official betrothal. I'm certain curiosity has them conjuring all sorts of interesting scenarios."

Biting back a disappointed sigh, Blaike also set about straightening her clothing. Everyone probably knew what was transpiring in the solarium. Nevertheless, Blaike needn't broadcast her indiscretion by returning to the drawing room rumpled.

As it always did, her curiosity demanded satisfaction, and she asked the question that had been tickling her tongue all evening.

"Oliver, has her ladyship offered you a position as well?"

Blaike stood and shook out her skirts, and after smoothing the satin with her hands, checked the pearls at her neck to make sure the clasp was in place at her nape.

"She has. Lady Sethwick quite likes my drawings and would like to commission me to oversee the building of a new clipper straightaway. However, I begged her indulgence until I settled a few matters."

"Come here, *amore mia*." He opened his arms

wide.

Blaike willingly stepped into his embrace once more. Her head resting on the firm expanse of his chest, her curves melding with his rigid lines, she fit there as if they were two halves of the same mold.

"How do you feel about a honeymoon in Italy, *cara*?"

Did he jest?

She arched away from him.

No. He appeared perfectly serious.

"Italy? Whyever would you go there?"

"Because, *amore,* I learned this very afternoon that amongst those documents you so wisely persuaded me to have translated, is a deed to a marble quarry and what looks—at least on paper—to be an extensive estate in Naples. It seems great-grandpapa didn't completely disinherit his adored daughter, after all."

Ah, that's why he'd been asking Heath about the fireplace. It was made of Italian marble. "Of course we should go. If that's what you wish."

"So much time has passed, the deeds might not be valid anymore. I know nothing of such matters. Naturally, I'll need to consult with a solicitor, here as well as in Italy." He lifted her chin, searching her eyes. The merest trace of vulnerability fringed the corners of his dear face. "You should know you are marrying a man who at this moment, owns nothing but an annoying cockatoo. All I have to offer you is my love, and I do so unreservedly."

"That's all I require, Oliver. I've never cared about possessions."

She wrapped her arms about his waist and hugged him tight. He was her everything. It would be enough to fall asleep with him at her side and wake to the same in the morn.

"Where you go, I go, Oliver. On a ship. In an apartment above your office. A hovel in the Himalayas or a mansion in Rome. All that matters is that we are together."

His head inched lower until his lips were but a hair's breadth away from hers.

"Blaike, *Il mio cuore è solo tua.*"

"My heart is yours too, Oliver."

Tilting her head and cupping his nape, she sealed her vow with a passionate kiss.

Fortunate is the woman who knows
this secret: for love to grow, she must risk
giving it away, so it may dwell and flourish in the
heart of the only person she trusts to keep it safe.

~Scruples and Scandals
The Genteel Lady's Guide to Practical Living

Epilogue

Naples, Italy
4 August, 1823

The entry's gold leaf grandfather clock peeled midnight as Oliver took the marble stairs two at a time.

His bride waited above, probably fast asleep given the late hour.

As he had since they'd arrived nearly two months ago, he marveled at the ostentatious mansion's architecture. It was quite the grandest, *gaudiest,* house he'd ever seen.

He and Blaike had gaped like country bumpkins upon crossing the threshold that first day. It hadn't taken them more than five minutes to decide this wasn't the place for them. Hence, Villa de Rossini had discreetly been put up for sale for a price that boggled but, which Signore Parodi, his solicitor, had insisted was quite fair.

The profitable quarry in Carrara Valley, Oliver opted to keep.

Pauper poor mere weeks ago, now he possessed wealth beyond anything he'd ever conceived. He and Blaike could have a home wherever they liked—France, Italy, even America—but she preferred to live near her family.

Wonder of wonders, he wanted to be near his, too.

Passing beneath his ancestors' gilded portraits, he paused at his great-grandsire, Francesco de Rossini's likeness.

Not a doubt who Abraham—not his real name— had descended from.

No, Lanzo Abramo Rossini possessed the same sly, close-set eyes and slightly sneering upper lip as his grandfather.

As vile as a dried horse turd in his mouth, the knowledge that Oliver was cousin to the knave who now called Newgate home stuck in his craw. Likely Abraham would remain imprisoned the rest of his days, unless his sentence was commuted to deportation to Australia instead.

Untying his neckcloth, Oliver continued down the corridor and yawned. He'd been up at dawn three days in a row.

The day Abraham torched *Nonno's* office, he'd been after the deeds to Villa de Rossini and the marble quarry.

His mother, the grand aunt who'd trotted off to England with her lover, had learned of the documents when her father died, and she'd returned home in disgrace for his funeral. She thought her bastard son was more entitled to the properties than *Mamma*. Or Oliver, another bastard and the only other remaining male in the family line.

Abraham had wrongly assumed the documents had been destroyed in the fire he set and never attempted to steal them again. He'd turned his festering disappointment into tormenting Oliver at every given opportunity.

Outside his chamber, Oliver paused, enjoying the peacefulness.

No screeching cockatoos.

M'Lady Lottie and her mate of six weeks, Michelangelo, were no doubt snuggled together on their perch in the conservatory. Neither would be pleased to leave their lush home, but another just as grand would be found for them in England.

Thirty servants staffed this great house. Yet the only sounds disturbing the tranquility were the whisper of a mild breeze caressing the sheer panels covering open windows as well as crickets' and cicadas' songs filtering from the balconies on this side of the manor.

Before Oliver lowered the latch, he also said a quiet prayer of thanks for the entrancing woman beyond the door.

Seems Hawkins's faith had at long last borne fruit.

The angry bitter man Oliver had once been had been replaced by one who daily gave thanks for the many undeserved blessings bestowed upon him.

Quietly opening his bedchamber door, his heart swelled behind his breastbone. He'd never tire of seeing that vision.

Blaike, her wondrous hair spilling over her shoulders, wearing nothing but a sleeveless nightgown, lying in their bed, waiting for him.

She gave him a drowsy smile and held her arms open in invitation. "You're later than I thought you'd be, darling."

After an embrace and a hungry kiss that promised more, he divested himself of his boots.

"That's because, *cara mia,* Signore Parodi found a buyer for this monstrosity. A duke, no less. He wishes to take possession before the end of August, if you're in agreement."

"I'd like that. I haven't hardly seen Blythe's darling Effie yet, and Brette is due any day."

"I'm done in, I tell you. Tomorrow, I refuse to rise before seven." In a few quick movements, Oliver divested himself of the rest of his clothing.

Blaike's welcoming smile turned seductive as she perused his naked form. His wife wasn't the least inhibited, and in fact, after finding a naughty book from the seventeenth century in the library, had made several creative suggestions regarding their love play.

"I think," she said, trailing her fingertips along the bottle green satin sheet, "I shall take up painting. Just so I can have a nude likeness of you to peek at whenever I please."

Smothering another yawn, he edged between the sheets. The other bedcoverings had been turned back to the foot of the bed due to the room's summer heat.

"*Bella,* I've seen your attempts at drawing, and I fear I'd resemble a troll. You'll just have to be satisfied with seeing me in the flesh."

"*Hmph,* if you weren't so dashed attractive, I'd be offended. But then again, you make a valid point. I possess abysmal artistic abilities."

Blaike came willingly into his arms, laying her shiny head upon his shoulder and placing a smooth-as-satin milky white leg upon his hair-covered thigh. The emerald and diamond ring, now sized to fit her ring finger, sparkled in the candlelight.

Drawing lazy circles on his chest, she kissed his shoulder,

"I had a most interesting letter from Blythe today. The Severs have been chased back to America in disgrace by their brother-in-law, Lord Desmond. Seems they were found in a compromising situation." She swirled his chest hair with her forefinger even as he caressed a velvety buttock. "With each other, no less."

"Never say so." Oliver couldn't keep the shock from his voice.

Sailors saw and heard many things that would appall respectable society, but even he hadn't encountered that particular perversion.

"Good riddance, I say, even if Ravensdale and the others essentially had already banished them to *le Beau Monde's* outermost fringes because of what they did to you."

"Oliver?" Blaike raised up on her elbow, the white waterfall of her hair billowing onto his torso.

"Yes, *amore*?" Hand on her trim waist, he edged her higher until she lay upon him, their legs tangled beneath the mussed sheet. His manhood's gradually swelling suggested that perhaps he wasn't so very tired after all.

Her mouth a mere inch from his, she flicked her pink tongue out to lick her lower lip.

"I read an interesting passage in *The Ladies' Delight* this evening that I should very much like to attempt." She gave him a wide-eyed look, seductress and innocent combined. "If you aren't too tired, darling, that is."

"*Cuore mio*, my heart, I shall never be too tired, as long as I have breath in my lungs and blood flowing through my veins to show you how much I love you."

Want a FREE first in series Starter Library
from Collette?

Go to: signup.collettecameron.com/TheRegencyRoseGift
to get a five FREE book bundle.

THE LIEUTENANT AND THE LADY

The Culpepper Misses, Book Five

How can he choose between duty and the woman he'd give his life for?

When Blaire Culpepper returns to England, she hopes to finally declare her love to dashing Lieutenant Julian Drake. Except, in her absence, he's inherited his brother's estate, sold his commission, and has been courting another woman. According to the rumor mills, a marriage announcement is expected any day.

From the moment Julian laid eyes on Blaire many month ago, she entranced him. But as soldier far beneath her station, he battled his growing fascination. When his brother dies, Julian social status changes. But so does his newfound intentions of courting Blaire and winning her hand…

Circumstances and honor have forced him into considering a union with another woman. But that means breaking Blaire's heart and his own as well…

About the Author

USA Today Bestselling author COLLETTE CAMERON® is renowned for her Scottish and Regency historical romance novels featuring daring rogues, scoundrels, and the strong heroines who capture their hearts. Her stories are filled with inspiration and humor, making them the perfect escape for fans of Sweet-to-Spicy Timeless Romances®. Living in Oregon, Collette is a confessed Cadbury chocoholic and dreams of spending part of her time in Scotland. From the rugged highlands to the refined drawing rooms of Regency England, Collette's stories transport you to another time and place, where love and adventure are just a page away.

Dearest Reader,

Blaike and Oliver's story truly started in *The Marquis and the Vixen*, but I had to wait until Blaike was a tad older to set her romance in motion. I wanted their tale to be slightly different than the first three Blue Rose Regency Romances: The Culpepper Misses books, and since Oliver was a sea captain, I decided the *Sea Gypsy* would make the perfect setting for a large portion of their story.

As my characters always do, Oliver and Blaike directed their story, and the twists they came up with never failed to surprise me. He proved to be a much more complex character than I'd first anticipated, and M'Lady Lottie turned out to be a great deal of fun, too. I hope you enjoyed her antics.

You'll see Blaire's story in the very near future as well.

Please consider telling other readers why you enjoyed this book by reviewing it at Amazon, Goodreads, Apple, or Barnes & Noble. Not only do I truly want to hear your thoughts, reviews are crucial for an author to succeed. **Even if you only leave a line or two, I'd very much appreciate it.**

Here's wishing you many happy hours of reading, more happily-ever-afters than you can possibly enjoy in a lifetime, and abundant blessings to you and your loved-ones.

Collette Cameron

Printed in Great Britain
by Amazon

36322988R00163